Tangled Tail

A Madelaine Jones Mystery

Susan Williamson

Cactus Mystery Press
An imprint of Blue Fortune Enterprises, LLC

Cactus Mystery Press Titles by Susan Williamson

Madeline Jones Mysteries:

Desert Tail
Tangled Tail

Cozy Mysteries:

Dead on the Trail

TANGLED TAIL

For information contact :
Blue Fortune Enterprises, LLC
Cactus Mystery Press
P.O. Box 554
Yorktown, VA 23690
http://blue-fortune.com

Book and Cover design by Wesley Miller, WAMCreate, wamcreate.co

ISBN: 978-1-948979-08-5

First Edition: September 2018

Dedication

To my brother, John Ringling North II,
who continues to light up my life.

ONE

CRASH! BANG! THE tinkle of shattering glass echoed through the house. I froze, then grabbed the phone from my desk and crept toward the kitchen. The two dogs charged down the hall almost knocking me over. I stopped. Silence, then a solitary thud. I jumped, caught my breath, and resumed my stealthy steps.

The kitchen floor was a sea of broken dishes. After last year's horror, I always made sure to keep doors and windows locked. They remained intact, but the bottom dishwasher rack was amongst the carnage. One of the dog's collars must have caught on a prong. He or she had panicked.

Damn. I had just bought that stoneware set at a thrift store last week, and I really liked it.

Adrenaline surges make me hungry. Stepping around the mess, I sank into a chair and grabbed a banana from the fruit bowl.

I twitched as the phone in my hand rang. The number was unfamiliar but had a lot of digits. It might be Simon. Was he in Ireland on Garda duties or elsewhere on a secret mission? I answered with my mouth full of banana. "Hello?"

"Hello, Maddie, are you there? Maddie, you sound strange. Are you all right?"

I swallowed before I said, "Simon, I'm fine. The dogs just pulled out my dishwasher rack and broke everything—but we're okay."

My chocolate Lab, Katie, and my stepmother's labradoodle, Dipsy, were now slinking back down the hall toward the catastrophe that one or both had caused. Not wanting to deal with injured paws, I blocked the dogs with my leg.

"Can I call you back?"

"I'll call you," he said. "Is thirty minutes good?"

"Great."

I took the dogs to the bedroom and inspected them for cuts and scrapes. They were unblemished. I removed Dipsy's choke collar and rubbed his neck. He seemed to be okay, if a little nervous.

I locked them in the bedroom, much to their displeasure. With a broom and dustpan from the hall closet I headed back to the mess. I gingerly picked up the big pieces and swept the shards. Then I vacuumed to be sure broken china wouldn't end up in my feet or their paws.

Forty minutes had gone by—Simon should be calling. I calculated the time difference from Ireland. I missed him, but I had been busy remodeling a low country cottage that Jane Best owned and working on her horse farm near Charleston, South Carolina. I could trade work for free rent and frequent riding opportunities. She offered me a deal that gave me sweat equity. If I wanted to buy the house later, she would consider my work as a down payment.

My phone conversations with Simon had felt comfortable. The relationship seemed to be growing more intimate even if we were living far apart.

An hour had passed. I knew that Simon might be caught up in a case and unable to call again for some time.

I puttered in the kitchen, fed the dogs, and fixed a sandwich. I tried to watch TV but couldn't follow the plot. Finally, I took a shower and put the dogs to bed. The phone woke me at five.

"Sorry, luv. I got tied up and couldn't call. Didn't want to wake you but might not have an opportunity later."

I tried to find my way through sleep fog. "It's okay, Simon. Good to hear your voice."

"And yours. Could you get away for a bit?"

My dad and stepmother would be home from their latest adventure by the weekend. Since I had kept Dipsy for two weeks, they owed me some dog sitting. The farm work was flexible. If I worked hard the next few days, Jane should be able to spare me. "I think so. What's up?"

"I'm coming to America next week on a case. Kentucky, actually. It involves horses. I need your expertise. And… I miss you."

"When and where, Commander?"

"Looks like Lexington, Kentucky, end of next week. I'll know more in a few days."

I was wide awake now. Yes. I was ready to be with Simon again and see if our relationship would progress without the adrenalin-filled nightmare of last winter and spring. My deep depression after losing my husband in Afghanistan had literally been exploded away along with my house and most of my possessions.

Simon had come into my life, and saved it more than once, when a case he was working on overlapped my quest for the truth of what had happened to Jim. Over the months we had fallen in love in spite of both of our efforts not to get involved. I had last seen him at the preliminary trial in July, and now it was October.

"I can drive, so we won't need to rent a car." I went on to tell him about the house.

"I'll be in touch, have to go now."

I got dressed and let the dogs out, eager to be at work and make the time pass quickly.

***

I found a space in short term parking and hurried into the Lexington airport. Bluegrass Field had grown since my graduate school days in Kentucky, but it was still surrounded by fields of grazing horses. I had expected Simon's case to be dealing with Thoroughbreds, but the man he was investigating owned American Saddlebred show horses, not race horses. He was importing them via Ireland to the United States from South Africa where they had been a fixture since the 1930s.

The monitor showed Simon's plane from JFK running late. I took a deep breath and went to the restroom. I gave myself a critical look as I straightened my windblown hair and applied lipstick. I was eager to see Simon again and suddenly nervous. What if things weren't what I expected? What if he was no longer interested in a romantic relationship, or the chemistry was gone?

I grabbed coffee and a donut and sat to read where I could see the arrivals area. After reading the same page five times, I got up to stretch.

There he was, scanning the room for me, dressed in his impeccable tweeds. He smiled as we made a beeline for each other.

Simon cupped my face in his hand before kissing me soundly. "You look great, luv. I'll get my other bag. Do you mind if we to go straight to the Kentucky Horse Park? The horses just cleared quarantine in New Jersey. They're being shipped here to join the rest of his trainer's show string."

I went to get the truck. Simon was at the curb with his luggage when I drove up. He watched the traffic turning into Keeneland Racetrack across the road as we exited the airport. "That looks like a fun outing. Lovely track, there."

"It is, but it has lost some of the ambiance of years ago. 'Racing the way it was meant to be,' was their slogan. In those days, they didn't even have a loudspeaker. You could walk right up to the horses being saddled in the paddock. I used to pretend I was an owner."

We drove a short distance and hit New Circle Road, then Newtown Pike, heading north toward the park. Showplace farms with miles of black or white board fencing dotted the landscape.

Simon told me about the case. "We're pretty sure this man is moving large sums of money from one country to another, but we can't find it. We suspect he's shipping arms out of Ireland into Africa, but we can't find a payment trail. Thought the show horses would be a good cover for money laundering, but we can't figure the system. That's why I need you, Maddie. You might be able to spot something that doesn't fit."

I laughed. "Money going down the drain, you mean. Plenty of opportunity for that in the show horse world."

"Curtis Monkton, The Fifth Earl of Clairemont, is a British subject, raised in South Africa, with a farm in County Clare, Ireland. He has his American show horses with Piet De Wet, originally South African. Do you know him?"

"No. But new South Africans keep arriving. The economy is so bad there that they pretty much have to come to America if they want to make it in the horse business."

"This trainer didn't have any opening for farm help, but Joe got a job doing maintenance for the Horse Park. He's been here a week."

Joe Mundi often served as Simon's eyes and ears on the ground and could blend into lots of different situations. I would be glad to see him again and find out what appearance he had adopted this time.

Simon sent Joe a text as we pulled onto the show grounds. My old farm truck looked right at home. Joe suggested Simon meet him at the barn area restroom where Joe was emptying trash. I visited the Ladies' while Simon entered the Mens'.

I walked out and surveyed the action around me. The show didn't start until the next evening, so trainers and grooms were busy setting up their tack rooms, clipping, washing, and working horses. Some barns were still unloading and golf carts zipped in and out among tractor-trailers sporting colorful farm logos or commercial hauling names.

I found De Wet's stalls about the same time a commercial van came to a stop beside them. The trainer called a groom to assist in unloading the horses. The first horse to step down the ramp was a lovely bay mare. She was unshod, so I assumed she was one of the horses coming out of quarantine. They would have pulled off her show shoes for safety before she boarded the plane in South Africa.

De Wet issued detailed instructions to the groom going for the second horse. "Be sure to put the chain over his nose and don't get near another horse."

The stallion jumped down the ramp, pulling the hapless groom behind him. When he hit the ground he whirled and kicked, just missing the groom at the end of his lead. De Wet yelled, "Shorten the lead and give him a jerk or you'll lose him."

The groom got his feet solidly underneath him and pulled the horse's head back to him. "Whoa, straighten up."

The chaos had attracted a crowd. There was no doubt the horse was magnificent. He put his heels in the air again and squealed. With another sharp tug on the lead, the groom managed to get the horse moving forward, and they jogged toward the open stall door.

The other groom ran to fill water buckets with the hose and bring hay to the new horses. I caught De Wet's eye. "That's quite a horse."

"We'll see what he is. His name is Rooibos Commander. His own groom is coming tomorrow, I'm glad of that." One trunk was unloaded along with the horses and carried back to the stable's work tack stall. I was sure it had been inspected many times during the journey from South Africa.

I couldn't stay any longer without looking suspicious, so I walked back toward the restroom and found Simon. "I doubt we'll learn anything until his groom arrives in the morning."

We found a diner and ordered meatloaf and other comfort food while Simon filled me in. "Joe hasn't had time to learn much, only that De Wet seems to be well thought of by most of the other trainers and grooms. The new horse was a South African champion and was bought at a high price—between $750,000 and $900,000—he heard several figures. He'll give us a call if the groom shows up before we do."

On the way to the motel, Simon was focused on his case, but he was as easy to be with as when we had parted. He changed gears and asked in detail about Sanda, one of the Turkmen girls we had rescued last summer. I had jumped through all the hoops necessary to become a foster parent, and she would soon be coming to live with me.

"How have you been?" I asked, as we turned into the motel lot and parked.

He looked over at me and pulled me close. "More lonesome. I really did miss you. My life was busy enough, but now there is a void that was partly filled with the knowing of you but not the having of you. In a way like a toothache that gets worse when you prod it."

I burst out laughing. "A toothache? I might have been called worse, but not lately."

Simon had the sense to look sheepish. "Sorry, luv, not much sleep lately. Let's get our room and take care of that."

And we did. Eventually.

***

I woke Simon with my screams. I was back in Turkmenistan, in the awful barren graveyard. Instead of Jim's grave, I saw his body, crimson staining his chest as he reached for me. Someone had a hold of my other hand, pulling me away.

"He's gone, Maddie."

I struggled and sobbed as I tried to breathe.

TWO

"**MADDIE, WAKE UP**. You're safe." Simon attempted to pull me into his arms, but I pushed him away until I woke up and realized where I was.

I stopped fighting him and gulped air. "Jim was dead, but he was reaching for me out of the grave. I couldn't save him, I couldn't do anything. Turkmen girls called for me from a panel truck, and I couldn't save them either."

Simon pulled me close and rubbed my back. "Maddie, I'm so sorry. And you did do something. You found the truth and helped to catch those responsible. I love you, you know. But if it's too soon for us to be together..."

"No, Simon. I want to be with you. But it was so real."

"Breathe. I'm here. It was a nightmare. Hush now."

He kept rubbing my back, and my breathing slowed as I cuddled against him.

The alarm buzzed all too early. We needed to see if the South African groom had arrived. Complimentary coffee and donuts near the horse show office caught our eye on the way to the barn. Simon looked the part in his jeans, boots, sweater, and ball cap. It was quiet at the barn, so we walked back to watch the horses working in the arena, some being jogged, others ridden and a few long lined, until Simon got a text from Joe.

"The groom is here," Simon said. "He's met up with De Wet, and he's eager to work his horse."

We hurried to the barn. De Wet had added stall curtains completely covering the front of the stallion's stall. The new South African spoke to the other grooms. "I can get him ready. He doesn't like strangers, so best you stay out of his sight."

"Not to worry, Will," answered the poor groom who had unloaded the horse.

I had been thinking, between other activities, about how one could smuggle cash or more likely diamonds from South Africa via a horse. You could hide something between a horse's foot and shoe if he were wearing protective pads, but his shoes and pads had been removed before he was shipped. I doubted if anyone got too close to this particular animal's tail. When he was putting his heels in the air yesterday, I noticed that he had a thick tail, tightly braided.

I motioned to Simon to follow me, and we moved to the block of stalls directly behind De Wet's. Luckily, no one was around. I squatted behind a tack trunk, pretending to adjust my boot in case anyone came along. Will spoke softly to the horse as he snapped the cross ties to his halter. The stallion turned his head, trying to nip as Will pulled off his blanket. The groom began to brush the horse, keeping close to his body and a careful eye on his hindquarters. He took hold of the stallion's massive tail, pulled it to the side and commenced to unwrap and unbraid it.

De Wet came up to the stall. "You all right there, Will?"

"I'm good, but keep everyone away till I've gotten him ready, yeah? I need to redo his tail. It's a right tangle."

"Okay. You know how he ticks, or how he kicks, I should say."

Simon snapped pictures as Will unbraided the tail, but since there was a horse and stall boards between us, we couldn't see much. A folder rested on a trunk outside the stall next to us. "I've got an idea."

I grabbed the folder and started at the end of the stalls on the far side of the stallion. I pulled out a proof of a Coggin's test—all horses had to have one, and someone was likely to be inspecting to see that the horses had tested negative for equine infectious anemia. We pretended to be checking the first horse. "This one's right. Let's check the next." We worked our way down the stalls. Fate was in our favor, the horse behind the stallion wore leg wraps. "Better take a closer look at this one."

Just then a groom walked up. "Could you hold him and let us see his leg markings?" I asked. He grabbed a lead and clipped on the horse's halter while I bent and looked at the leg markings. That's when Will unbraided a small section of tail and dropped something into his pocket. "Better get a picture of his rear markings," I said, "so they'll know we checked everything." I stepped between the groom and Simon while he snapped pictures of the activity in the adjoining stall. "We'll check that one later."

With that we moved into the next barn. I quickly put on my sunglasses and pulled a cap out of my pocket, shrugging off my jacket as we walked. Simon started to laugh. "Well done, Miss Hari. Not sure how much I caught on video, but he was definitely taking something out of that horse's tail."

He quickly texted Joe, who was on trash pickup detail. Joe walked by the stall once, then returned as Will walked out and headed for the tack room. Joe managed to back into Will and knock him down, falling on top of him. "So sorry, sir. I wasn't looking. I didn't know you were behind me."

Will rolled over and got up, brushing himself off. "No problem. Could happen to anyone."

I had moved into the dark restroom door and watched from there. Will checked his pockets as he stood up. Satisfied, he turned again toward the tack room. Simon had walked down the barn aisle and stopped to look at a horse next to the tack room. Will came out without his jacket, carrying long lines and a bridle.

I joined Simon outside the barn. Joe texted him that there were stones in Will's pocket, and Joe had palmed one. Hard to tell, but it looked to be a small, rough diamond.

There was no way for any of us to inspect the tack room without causing suspicion so we walked to the next barn. As badly as I wanted to see the horse work, I knew we needed to try to get to Will's jacket. De Wet's other grooms had returned from working horses and were busy putting horses away and tacking up others. No one left long enough for us to have a look, and then Will and Rooibos were returning. The horse was dancing as he walked, hot from the work but not appearing a bit tired.

We gave up on getting in the tack room for the moment. If Will had stashed diamonds there, he wouldn't be leaving them. Joe had managed to put a tracker on Will's truck, and we would know if he left the show grounds. Walking back toward the arena, Simon paused as we neared the Parade of Breeds conducted daily by the Kentucky Horse Park.

He looked toward the entry gate and nudged me. "Isn't that one of the Turkmenistan horses there?"

A beautiful Akhal-Teke stood quietly, horse and rider garbed in traditional costume which included silver collars around the horse's neck. I tried to decide what color the horse was. His coat gleamed metallic silver with a hint of gold dapples underneath. His mane and tail were black.

"Yes, in full costume, too. Funny we never saw one outfitted like that in Turkmenistan." The search for the truth about my husband's death had led us to that fascinating country the previous winter. As much as I loved Saddlebreds, I was also in love with the Tekes. We watched as he trotted into the ring, head held high and legs extended. After his performance, we continued to the show ring concessions for coffee then returned to the barn.

As we passed the barn, Will walked out of the tack room with his jacket and jogged toward the lot where Joe had told us Bill's truck, an old blue F-150, was parked. Will turned suddenly and walked toward us. We nodded and kept walking. Joe followed him, leaving the barn area and walking toward the Saddlebred Museum. Simon took after them at a distance, and I ran to get my truck. I picked Simon up just as Will got into the passenger side of a black Range Rover parked in the general admission lot. We hid behind a line of cars near the entrance.

Joe called. Simon turned toward me. "He's getting out, and the vehicle is leaving. Let me follow the Range Rover while you watch Will."

I slid out of the truck and Simon came around to the driver's side. Will jogged back in the direction of the horse barns. I walked beside the arena and make-up ring, watched a horse work, and ambled to the stables. Activity was winding down now. Trainers were leaving for lunch or a nap before the pre-show activities started. Will helped the other grooms wash a few horses then walked again to his truck. As he got closer, a heaviness settled over me. I walked toward him but didn't know what I would say. The unease was coalescing into dread and a vision of flames. He unlocked the truck door with his remote, and my phone rang. He didn't notice me as he opened the truck door and started to climb into the driver's seat.

My father's number appeared on the phone screen, and I answered. "Maddie," he yelled, "get back."

"Will, no," I yelled. "Don't get in."

He looked at me as if I had lost my mind, got in and inserted his keys in the ignition. But he hesitated before he cranked the engine.

"I think there's a bomb, don't start it."

"What the hell? Who are you?" He sat for a minute looking at me and then eased out of the truck. "What do you know?"

He wouldn't be likely to credit my father's psychic talent and my own vision of disaster. But I firmly believed that Will would be history if he started that truck. My father had saved my life before with his warning, and I knew it was real. "You don't know me, but I think you're in danger."

He grabbed my arm. "We'll see. Get in the truck."

My dad's voice was still coming from my phone. "Maddie, are you all right?"

Will grabbed the phone and let go of my arm. "Who are you, and what do you know about my truck?"

I was tempted to run, but that wouldn't save Will, and I didn't want his life on my conscience. I backed away a few steps while he listened. Finally, he squatted down and looked under the truck. He stood up and walked back to me, holding out the phone. "I see a wire. Talk to him. I won't hurt you."

"Thanks, Dad. We're away. I'm safe. Simon will be along shortly." I immediately texted Simon to come quickly.

Will looked at a bench on the edge of the grass. "Let's sit down. What's this about? Who are you?"

"I'm just a horse fan and a little psychic. But my friend—he can tell you more. He'll be here in a minute." I hoped that was true. But Joe watched from a distance then moved closer. So I thought I was safe enough.

Simon drove up in my truck and stopped near the bench. He raised his eyebrows and looked at us.

"We think there's a bomb under his truck."

"Your dad?" Simon had learned that my father's premonitions were real.

I nodded. "And I had my own twinge."

Will looked out in the distance while he clenched and unclenched his fist, then picked at a nail.

Simon parked and came back to us. "Do you want us to call the police? Do you have any idea why someone would bomb your truck?"

"No. Please. No."

Simon pulled out his ID. "I can try to help you, but I have to know everything."

"You're Irish? What are you doing here?"

"Let's just say we've been following the diamonds and go from there."

Will's face paled and sweat beaded on his forehead, despite the cool morning.

"I—I had to do a favor for someone. I thought I was finished. I thought it was over. My wife is still in South Africa. They threatened her. They said they'd get her and hurt Rooibos if I didn't do as they asked. My dad and I raised this horse. I've spent half my life making him what he is. We still own half-interest in him. I was a trainer back there—when there were more people to pay training."

"Who are they?"

"I have no idea. Just got emails about what to do, what would happen if I didn't. The diamonds were delivered to our barn in Bloemfontein, before I left with the horse. I had to braid them into his tail. Spent two months in Ireland and then the horses were shipped to America. I gave the stones to a guy in a black car. Breathed a sigh of relief, you know? But if there's a bomb in my truck..."

"No one is safe. Is your boss the one who asked you to do this?"

"Lord Monkton? No. Of course not. I mean, at least I don't think so." Will looked from one of us to the other. "What about my wife? And the horse? They'll not be safe either."

"If they think you're out of the way, they won't likely bother with either. We need to go ahead and explode your truck. You don't by any chance have a remote start on that thing, do you?"

"Actually, I do. Came with it. B-b-but it's on the key ring—in the truck."

"We could leave it and let a local car thief suffer the consequences, but I reckon that's a little steep punishment for some kid who might just want to joy ride. I'll need a long stick," Simon said as he looked around.

We walked back to the barn and gathered a lunge whip and a rake. Simon tied the whip to the rake and fashioned a piece of wire into a hook on the end of the whip. He gently opened the passenger side truck door and backed away, easing the contraption across the seat. My heart was in my throat, and I prayed earnestly. On the second try, the keys slid out and Simon retrieved them.

Fortunately, no one was parked close. We got in my truck and drove to the end of the lot. Simon handed the keys to Bill. "Gentlemen, start your engines."

Will climbed out of the truck and faced his vehicle. His hand shaking, he glanced at Simon, who nodded encouragement. Will pushed the button.

At first, nothing happened. I held my breath and began to let it out just as a blast shook the area. Flames shot into the air and debris rained down. I had a terrifying flashback, remembering my house in flames—Simon realized and reached for me. "So sorry, luv, shouldn't have let you watch."

Will collapsed against my truck door and stood motionless, sweat drenching his face. The grooms and trainers who were still around ran toward the burning truck, several stopping to call 911, others shooting video with their phones. We walked toward the inferno, but kept to the back of the crowd.

Park fire officials responded first, followed by a two Lexington trucks and police cars. Officers waved everyone back and asked if anyone knew the owner of the truck. No one did. As the foam quieted the fire, we walked slowly back to my truck and drove away.

Simon made calls to South Africa, asking for protection for Bill's family. He told Joe to keep an eye on De Wet's stable.

Will was a nervous wreck. He wanted to be back home protecting his wife and at the barn protecting his horse, mutually exclusive activities, but Simon assured him he could do the most good by sharing everything he knew in our hotel room.

Simon had followed the Range Rover to a shopping mall where the driver entered, made contact with someone, and quickly left. The diamonds were en route to wherever. If they were being used for arms shipments, the shipments must be originating in the United States rather than Ireland, or why would they wait until the horses came to America before collecting? Will said he was originally told to remove the stones in Ireland, which he did, but an email told him to hide them again and take them out in Lexington.

Lord Monkton was to arrive the next day. Would he expect to find Will alive and well at the stable?

THREE

THE PLAN WAS for De Wet to meet Monkton at the airport when his chartered jet arrived. Will volunteered, told the trainer he had something he wanted to tell the owner about his time in Ireland. De Wet was okay with that, and Will told him that his truck was in the shop—fortunately De Wet didn't know whose truck had exploded. Will would drive the stable truck, and we would take mine.

We parked at the far end of the lot and walked separately to the terminal. We stood on opposite sides of the charter jet entrance to the terminal. Either Monkton was a good actor, or he knew nothing about the attempt on Will's life. He greeted Bill with a handshake and handed over his luggage. They walked toward the parking lot, deep in conversation.

***

Will held the pawing, fretting stallion while the show farrier tacked on his shoes. Monkton walked down the stable row with De Wet, discussing each of his horses.

They decided to go ahead and work Rooibos under saddle. The blacksmith wanted to see if his shoes needed adjusting. Will led him out and slid a blinker hood over his full bridle. De Wet held the horse with one hand over the horse's nose and another on the snaffle rein as Will vaulted into the saddle, gathering his reins when the magnificent animal stepped forward.

Rooibos was attracting a lot of attention and several people followed him to the show ring. The horse was a tightly woven spring, prancing, occasionally bucking and leaping toward the arena. Will dropped his hand to the horse's withers, speaking softly. The stallion leapt through the gate and took off racking when Will tried to restrain him. But what a rack—his feet didn't appear to touch the ground, and his stride was enormous. Will circled to slow him and then turned the horse loose to trot. His trot was equally impressive, pushing off his hocks and taking huge steps. A country pleasure horse ducked his tail and spooked sideways when Will roared past him. Rooibos started to kick but Will anticipated by lifting the snaffle and using the whip in his outside hand.

Simon had never seen a horse like this, few of us had. We stood mesmerized. Only when the horse was covered with lather and breathing hard did Will bring him to the center and ask him to stand. De Wet and Monkton were smiling. Will was catching his breath. The challenge was rating this horse, keeping him under control. No wonder Will was part of the package.

Simon glanced at his phone and walked away. I looked around to see if anyone in the arena had watched the stallion work. A janitor pushed a broom at the top of the stands. As I turned back to Will a loud pop echoed in the arena. Will slumped forward. Rooibos was off like a rocket. A figure ran down the far steps, and Simon took off after him. De Wet, the farrier, and I, as well as other trainers in the arena, tried to corner the galloping horse. Will was conscious and gathered the reins in his right hand as he leaned over the horse's neck. His efforts and ours slowed the horse enough that De Wet could grab the reins and bring him to a stop. Will slid off the horse, and the farrier helped him to the ground. Someone yelled for the paramedics and an ambulance.

Will was pale and sweating. "It's my shoulder—did someone bloody shoot me?" He struggled to sit up, but we insisted he lay still. De Wet took the agitated horse back to the barn. I stood there feeling useless. An EMT ran into the arena and an ambulance followed. The EMT cut away Will's shirt and began to apply pressure to a relatively small wound on the edge of his shoulder. "Tell Simon to check on my wife," he interrupted as the EMT attempted to question him.

By the time Simon returned, Will was in the ambulance, insisting he didn't need to go to the hospital and didn't have any insurance. Monkton said he would pick up the tab and that Will should be checked out. One of the EMTs spoke to Simon—he said the bullet scraped the groom, mostly a flesh wound but they would need to assess the damage at the emergency room.

An attempted shooting would merit police attention. Simon and I jumped in the truck to follow the ambulance to the Good Samaritan Hospital. Simon had not checked in with local authorities when he arrived in Kentucky. He doubted that Will would confess diamond smuggling to a local cop—that would probably land him in custody, and he wanted to be with his horse. I didn't understand all the ramifications of the case. Simon only shared on a need to know basis and I accepted that—as long as he told me what I needed to know.

We were able to join Will in the emergency room where the doctor eventually confirmed he was not in any danger. The bullet had raked out some flesh and a little muscle, but left no serious damage.

Simon asked Will if he had seen or recognized the shooter.

Will waited until all the medical personnel were out of earshot before answering. "It's got to be someone connected to the diamonds. But now my wife's not safe either. What am I to do?"

"I've got a few connections in your country. I've asked that your wife be moved to a safe place. And you might be safer too, if you went home."

"These blokes could find me anywhere, and I want to stay with my horse. I've invested half my life in making him. But I couldn't live if something happened to Elise."

"So, we've got to figure out who they are."

The doctor came in to talk to Will and agreed to release him to us if we would make sure he rested in bed. The cops showed up as we prepared to leave.

Simon saw them coming and left to get the truck. I told them I was a horse friend of Will's, here to take him back to his motel. They asked me to leave before they questioned him.

I read the out-of-date magazines in the waiting room. After thirty minutes an orderly wheeled him out to meet me. I called Simon, and he picked us up.

"I told them I'd no idea why someone shot at me. Technically I don't. After all, I did what they wanted."

"True enough. But they want to erase the evidence of what they've done."

We drove by a drugstore and picked up the prescribed painkillers for Will before meeting Joe at the motel where we helped the injured groom out of the car and into his hotel room. He was almost asleep when we tiptoed out the door, Simon keeping his room key card.

Simon called De Wet and asked to meet him and Lord Monkton at the horse park café. I expected to be there, but Simon insisted that I stay at the motel. "I promise I'll be back soon, and we'll grab dinner before the show starts."

An hour later he came to the room and fired up his laptop. After a while he shut it down and walked over to the bed where I was watching HGTV. "Ideas for your cottage?"

"Maybe. Wait, I've got pictures on my phone." I showed Simon the before and after shots of my house.

"Very nice." He took the phone out of my hand and put it on

the nightstand before leaning in to kiss me. "You might need to go home—I didn't think things would heat up this fast, and I want you safe. This isn't your deal."

"Simon." I took a deep breath and tried to control my emotions. "I realize I'm not a law enforcement officer, but we have worked in partnership before, and you asked for my help, not just my company, did you not?"

"True enough, but—"

"No 'buts'. If we're to be together, and you continue in this line of work, there will always be risks. To me and to you. I've bought in to that, and I believed you had as well. I want a life together, and I thought you did too." By now I was sobbing.

"Maddie, luv, I understand, and I'm trying to come to terms with it. But I want you safe, I can't help that." He lifted my chin to look at me. "I love you. I value your intelligence and your abilities." He stood up and walked to the window. "I won't send you away. But please promise you won't do anything without my knowing."

I smiled. "If you'll do the same. There will be some things you can't tell me. I understand. But tell me generally so I can understand."

Our truce and whatever may have followed it were interrupted by a frantic phone call from Will.

FOUR

"SLOW DOWN," SIMON said. "I can't understand you." He frowned as he listened. "We'll meet you at your room in ten." After disconnecting, he looked at me. "Will got an email about bringing the rest of the diamonds, as if he hadn't turned them all over to the guy in the Range Rover. Joe gave me one stone, but the email implied several were missing."

I shoved my feet into my boots and grabbed a jacket. "So who, how—"

"The black Range Rover belongs to a local, he was probably the shooter—does odd jobs for the Lexington crime lords. Didn't sound like that would be the smuggler. This proves it."

"I've heard of the 'Lexington Mafia', drugs, hot sheet hotels, and so on." Some of my Kentucky friends had clued me in to that, years ago when I was looking for a motel for a horse event.

"You do get around. Same group, I assume. Wonder if they were hired to pick up the stones or, if not, how they knew about them."

"Pillow talk? Hacking? Dishonor among thieves?"

After assuring himself that we were the ones knocking on his door, Will ushered us in. "I've no chance at all now."

I put my hand on Will's arm. "Sit, before you fall down."

He sagged to the bed, and Simon took the armchair. "Let's take it from the beginning. How did they first approach you in South Africa?"

"The first was rat poison. In a bag, tied outside Rooibos' stall. A note said, 'We are watching you, wait for instructions'."

"Did you consider going to the police?"

"Yeah, I considered it. But my country still has a lot of corruption, and I thought whoever was behind this might know if I did. I decided to wait and see what they wanted. Got an email that night. Had a picture of my wife hanging clothes in the garden. That scared me. Said all they needed was for me to take a small package with the horse. There had been a story in the local paper that the horse was sold and going to America."

"How long before you got the package?"

"A few weeks. We had to arrange transport for the horse. First to quarantine in South Africa, then Ireland, then the U.S. It was a few days before we left. I had even begun to relax—thinking maybe nothing more would come of it. Found the package in my groom box. Figured braiding the stones in his tail was the safest gamble, especially the way he kicks."

Will reached for an almost empty glass of water with a shaking hand.

"Here, let me get you more, or would you rather a Coke or something—there's a machine down the hall."

"I'd love a Coke, thanks."

"Simon?" He shook his head. I dug out some change and left them. I was back in a jiffy and didn't suppose I'd missed too much of the story.

"Said I'd be contacted in Ireland. I took his tail down once and redid it. Was afraid to put the stones anywhere else. Finally got an email saying they would pick them up in Kentucky. Sent another picture of my wife, in her car, out to go shopping."

"Was the first email you got here from the same address?"

"Sure, that's why I never thought to doubt it. I was anxious to get rid of the bloody things." He showed Simon the first message on his phone, telling him to meet someone in a black Range Rover near the Saddlebred Museum.

Simon studied the message before making notes in his laptop.

The second message was from the same address, dated two days later. It told Will to bring the diamonds to Keeneland for Saturday's races. He would be contacted when he got there.

"They'll kill my wife, my horse, and me—just to make a point."

"A point for whom—if none of you are around, who would be impressed?" Simon asked.

"For the next poor bugger they contact."

"We'd best show up with some diamonds then." He turned to me. "Does the university here have a geology department?"

"I'm sure they do."

He handed me the laptop as he got up to pace the room. I searched for the University of Kentucky department and faculty contact information. I found emails and phone numbers and determined that everyone had left for the day.

Joe arrived to stay with Will, and Simon ushered me out the door. "I believe I promised dinner before the show."

I suddenly realized I'd never had lunch, and I was starving. I knew just the place. Simon handed me the keys, and we headed east to Paris Pike and then to New Circle Road. The restaurant I remembered was still there, tucked in a small strip center.

The knotty pine walls sported race photos from years past. I encouraged Simon to order a "Hot Brown" while I did the same. The waitress brought draft beer in chilled glasses while we talked. Simon hadn't had time to tell me the gist of his conversation with De Wet and Monkton.

"I believe Lord Monkton is what he seems. He felt terrible about Will's injury and wants to help in any way. He promised protection for De Wet's stable. Despite the money he has now,

Monkton grew up rough. His father invested in South African mines and horses, lost a pile, and it was up to Monkton to restore the family fortunes. An aunt paved his way at Oxford, and he advanced his career using the family connections to launch a solid communications business. He spent a year or two working on South African horse farms and wants to aid the horse industry and people like Will."

The sandwiches arrived, crisp bacon and creamy cheese sauce covering roasted turkey on sour dough bread. Tangy coleslaw was the perfect side dish. I thought about what Simon had told me while I savored my dinner.

"Did you mention the arms trade that you suspect?"

"I did. But the more we both pondered the issue, the less sense it made. The surrounding African countries are trading diamonds for Chinese arms which are readily available. Information would make a better target."

"Are you talking government secrets, industrial espionage, or what?"

Simon drained his beer and looked at me. "That's the question, isn't it?"

We drove back to the Horse Park and watched the show. De Wet had a few horses showing. He rode a nice but unfinished three-year-old five-gaited colt, and one of his customers showed a leg waving, long-necked fine harness horse. They both made respectable shows and finished third and fourth in large classes.

I explained the divisions and standards to Simon as we watched. "Used to be, trainers rode the best horses. Now the amateurs do. They can afford to ride often, and they want the fun of showing the best horses. Several amateurs have even won World's Championships against trainers. Don't know how that plays out in South Africa."

The show ended around nine, and we headed back to the motel to check on Will and call it a night. It had been a very long day.

Will was even more upset than when we had left him. “They’ve sent another picture of Anise. You said she was safe.”

FIVE

SIMON STUDIED THE picture attached to the email. He transferred it to his computer and enlarged it. Then he smiled.

"You think it's funny, that they can find Anise?"

Simon took the laptop over to Will. Anise was walking down the street. Valentine advertisements appeared in the window behind her. "Take a close look, this is an old picture."

Will grabbed the computer, primed to argue. Then he relaxed. "I know this picture. Her sister made it when they were out shopping last winter. It was on my computer at home."

The idea stopped him. "This means they've hacked my bloody computer, too."

Simon paused for a minute. "Were any of your travel details in the story about the sale of the horse to Monkton?"

"No, just who bought him. There was also a story in the horse magazine. Right after our National Championship. Article said he was going to America. But no times or dates."

"Who arranged the shipping times?"

"Monkton did. And he notified me by my email—so my email was already hacked then?"

"Perhaps. But the information could have come from within

Monkton's organization as well. You need to get some sleep. Maddie, I'll bunk with Will. Let me walk you to the room."

That was fine with me. My bed was calling.

"You don't mind, do you? I don't think Will can sleep otherwise, and he's exhausted."

"I'm tired, too. And I need to talk with the geology department first thing tomorrow."

Simon opened the door and pulled me into a hug as we entered the room. "Sleep well, luv." He started to leave, then reached into his pocket and handed me a Blackberry. "Use this tomorrow for all of your calls. My new number is already on it."

I looked at him in confusion. "New number?"

"Older technology. More secure. Wouldn't do for anyone to know we're looking for fake diamonds."

I was able to talk with a geology professor by eight-thirty the next morning. He had office hours before his eleven o'clock class and invited me over. Since I was familiar with the UK campus, my graduate alma mater, I volunteered to go while Simon hung out at the horse barn.

Parking near campus was every bit as bad as I remembered it. But I finally found a space on the street only a few blocks away from the geology department. Professor Bartley was in his mid-thirties, casual and friendly. I told him I needed a bag of stones that would be similar to weight and texture to rough diamonds. I explained it was for a magazine exposé. And it well might be, eventually.

He walked over to a locked closet. "I think I have just the thing. I do a gemstone ID project in one of my classes, and I give the students lots of samples." He pulled out a felt bag and inserted several stones until I decided the weight and amount looked about right.

"Are these valuable in their own right? I mean, do I need to give you a deposit or something?"

"I can find plenty more. No deposit needed for a fellow graduate. But I insist that you tell me the whole story later. And you need to sign a lease form."

"Fair enough, Dr. Bartley. Thank you very much."

I hid my loot under the seat and headed back to the horse park.

Will was feeling better and had insisted on coming to the barn to supervise the work of his horses. De Wet himself jogged the bay mare and long-lined Rooibos. We watched from the bleachers.

Simon told me the latest. "I've contacted the local FBI, we're meeting this afternoon. I'll need more help at Keeneland."

As a civilian, I would not be welcome at that meeting. I was glad to hang out at the barn and help if I could.

I was in the grandstand watching when Simon made it back. "They're going to assist. References from Charleston gave me credibility." The finale to a case targeting human traffickers had played out in federal court in Charleston last summer.

"What's the plan?"

"They're formulating it as we speak. I should know tonight." I gave him the fake stones, and he added the real diamond Joe had pickpocketed earlier.

"I was thinking. One of my friends from graduate school married a local Thoroughbred trainer. They might have stalls at Keeneland."

"That could come in handy. Maybe you can find out tonight."

We snacked on beer and brats from the arena concession stand. Joe took a tired Will back to the motel. The Feds called around ten, and Simon walked outside to take the call. He returned when the show ended, and we hurried out to get the truck.

"I'm going with the Feds in the morning. Will should be getting detailed instructions tonight. Joe can take him to the track. Let's see if we can find your friends online, and then we'll finish our plan."

I didn't know if I was to be part of the plan or not. But a fall

Saturday at the Keeneland races was too good to miss.

***

I'd finally found my friends' horse farm online and a phone number. Sally said she'd meet me for breakfast at the track kitchen, so I planned to drive out early. Simon was a part of whatever the Feds were planning for the diamond delivery, but he was not at liberty to explain it to me, and I understood.

As early as I was, there was very little traffic. The air was cool and crisp, and the trees wore full color for the occasion. I had chosen my best jeans, boots, and a sweater for the day, thinking about the expensive suits and hats that would be worn in the clubhouse. I parked as close to the barns as I could and hurried toward the track kitchen.

Sally was as blonde and beautiful as I remembered.

We reminisced over eggs and bacon. "I remember how you used to stay with me, and I would beg you to make breakfast," she said.

I laughed. "After crashing at your place with my dog, it was the least I could do."

Her son, who I remembered as a toddler, was now a teenager. He was at the barn with his dad getting their horse ready for the fourth race. He would pony the three-year-old to the gate.

I explained why I was in town, but without all the details. Sally wasn't aware of Jim's death and felt badly. And she wanted to know all about Simon.

My phone dinged with a text. Will is to bring the package to barn C after the fifth race. We'll be on foot. I chased an idea. "Sally, any chance I could borrow your outrider pony after the race?"

"Want to ride around Keeneland? As long as you stay away from the track itself, it should be fine. He's a good fellow. I raised him out of my old Quarter Horse mare."

I wasn't really planning on a trail ride around the premises, although that would certainly be enjoyable. Mounted back-up might be useful.

Should I suggest that to Simon or not? Remembering how some things we hadn't told each other turned out in the past, I decided to go with full disclosure.

Will be on horseback as backup. Will not interfere unless needed.

SIX

MY PHONE RANG. Simon wasn't as negative as I had expected. Once I explained how and where I was getting the horse, he thought it might be good if I rode by, but not too close. I was absolutely not to go after any bad guys—only to observe, possibly lend my horse—depending on what happened.

Over coffee refills, I explained more to Sally. Asked if it was okay if Simon or I had to take off on the horse. I assured her that we would be responsible if anything happened, although I knew that nothing could replace a trusted equine.

"Maddie," she said, "I know you. If you think this is important, it is. And I can't wait to see this secret agent."

We ambled back to their barn, still catching up on our lives. Sally's husband, Dale, saw us approaching and grabbed me in a bear hug. "What are you doing not coming around for so long?" His red hair had faded but was more than compensated for by their son Bart's fiery curls.

I helped Sally groom a few horses and clean their stalls before Dale sent us back to watch the opening races. We went by the nearest betting window to each put ten dollars on a filly that Dale and Sally had bred and sold. She had won her last three races and was stepping up to steeper competition. Dale met us to watch the race.

Shewolf broke in the middle of the pack and stayed three horses back until the homestretch. Her jockey called on her, using the whip only once, and she charged through an opening to take the lead. We were all shouting when she crossed the finish line.

"That'll make her full sister worth a little more," Dale said.

Sally and I went to the window to collect before coming back to the barn. Their young horse was gleaming like newly minted copper, but Bart kept rubbing him. Moses, the Quarter Horse, was also shining. He wore a Western saddle and stood patiently cross tied. Dale bridled the race horse and sent Bart to lead Moses out.

"A Penny Saved is his name," Sally said. "He's the first horse we've bred that we kept long enough to race."

Sally held the colt while Dale shrugged into his navy blazer, then took the reins. The colt looked around and whinnied to his buddy. Bart swung onto Moses, and Dale handed the jittery colt off to him. We began the trip to the post. Sally had an extra pass to get me in the saddling enclosure. We watched Penny bounce around while Dale gave instructions to the jockey. The colt settled when the jockey approached him with the saddle. The colt stood quietly as the girth was tightened.

"He's really sensible," Sally said, "but this is his first race, so anything could happen."

She walked over and held the colt as Dale gave his jockey a leg up.

"I'll do my best, Mr. Wolf. I appreciate the chance."

"Just hope he does his best," Dale said as he gave the jockey a sendoff pat on the leg.

Bart took hold of the colt as the bugle blew, and they headed to the starting gate. Penny trotted briskly beside his stablemate, turning his head to see the crowd. He entered the gate like a pro. The bell rang. Penny charged smoothly out of the gate, not first, but not last. He switched leads as the jockey tipped him slightly toward the rail from his outside post position then settled into a steady gallop. His ears flicked back as another horse started by him, close on the outside. He dug in and increased his stride, losing the challenger. He was running second as they hit the homestretch, three lengths behind the leader. He made another charge but not enough to pass the winner.

Dale was grinning. "Good enough, Penny, good enough."

I was happy for my friends. I knew they worked hard and tried to do things the right way. No short cuts in this racing stable. I left them to congratulate the jockey and hurried back toward the stable area.

Dale and Sally were well liked, and a lot of other trainers shouted encouragement as they returned to the barn.

Bart handed me a helmet. "Mom's rules." He shortened the stirrups, and I climbed on the big bay gelding. He was as pleasant and well-mannered as I expected any horse of Sally's to be.

We took off walking. I enjoyed the sights from my new elevation. Moses and I moved away from the crowd and found a grassy stretch where we jogged and then loped under the trees. The fifth race was starting, so I rode by Barn C and planned my second approach.

Will hurried into sight, his hand in his right pocket. Simon wasn't in view, and I wouldn't recognize the Feds so I tried to be nonchalant.

Will didn't see me, which was a wonder since his neck was swiveling like a bobble head. I turned away, rode down the length of the barn, and then reversed, coming up about thirty feet behind Will. A slender man wearing a hat and sunglasses darted out of a tack room and approached him. Will handed off the bag and kept walking, looking straight ahead. A golf cart with two men sped around the corner, and, as it passed me, I noticed a gun in the passenger's hand.

I froze for a second and then dug my heels into Moses. Like his barrel horse ancestors, he launched himself forward, throwing me back in the saddle. I cut between the golf cart and Will and yelled, "Will, on your left, jump on." The cart slid to a stop to avoid the charging horse.

Will looked back and stepped sideways, then threw up his right hand. I hoped he could make it from there. I reached for his hand, and he vaulted onto the horse behind me. We dove around the corner of the barn and took off in the other direction. Simon and the Feds were walking quickly around the barn. They saw that I had Will and ran after the golf cart, one of them calling for backup.

We slowed to a walk when we reached the trees at the edge of the parking lot. Will looked around, then slid to the ground. He was massaging his injured shoulder.

"Are you okay? I hope that didn't hurt your shoulder."

"Not near as much as another bullet would. What the hell? There's no pleasing these buggers."

"Come on, follow me, we'll get you out of sight."

I rode back to the Wolf's barn and told Will to hide in the tack room until we heard from Simon.

I had started untacking the horse when Bart appeared. "Have a good ride? Looks like you opened him up a bit. He likes that."

I laughed. "He was good as gold. Thanks so much. Did you ever barrel race him?"

"Yeah, me and my buddy, we'd do all the local shows, you know rescue races and stuff. He was really good at that."

Still is, I thought, but decided not to share. I walked into the tack room with him and introduced Will as a Saddlebred groom from the show.

I checked my phone. Simon sent a message that the Feds had at least some of the bad guys, and he was on his way to the barn.

Bart offered us soft drinks and went back to putting up his horse.

He said his parents were with a customer in the stands.

Simon smiled as he walked toward me. He put an arm around my shoulder. "Good riding, Miss Oakley. Or was she better at shooting?"

"Not sure. Will's in there."

Sally and Dale came up next and asked me how my ride was. I introduced everyone and explained that Will needed to leave. I went to get the truck while Simon stayed. Sally volunteered to walk with me. I knew she had questions.

"So Mr. Secret Agent is ever so in love with you and a very sexy man. Are you two serious?"

"I hope so. I told him last summer that I needed time to think. In a regular life, not in the middle of an adrenaline fueled adventure. Yet here we are again in the middle of a case. But at least this time the case isn't about me.

"After he left I missed him, and I decided I was ready to move on. He is totally different than Jim, but I am in love, and I've finally stopped feeling guilty about it. But here we are, and we haven't had time to even talk, not really."

"Would you go to Ireland, or would he move here, or what?"

"I haven't a clue. That's why it's so complicated." I showed her his grandmother's ring, which I now wore on my ring finger. I'd moved my wedding band to my right hand.

"I think, if you have the chance to love again, you should always take it. But I know you're a lot like me—independent and not wanting to give up your life as it is."

"When I met Simon, I didn't have a life, only a cocoon of depression. I have to make sure I'm not overreacting to coming out of my funk. Another issue is that I have applied to foster one of the girls we rescued. I would like to adopt her. Simon is all for an eventual adoption as well. But I don't know about the international complications."

We climbed into the truck. Sally spoke as she fastened her

seat belt. "Dale and I had a rough patch a few years back. Some customers blackballed him, and we had to leave and go to a Quarter horse track in western Kentucky. He didn't do anything wrong, and his reputation and integrity were so important to him. He was in a deep hole. It was horrible. I almost left, not because I couldn't handle the hard times, but because I couldn't bear to see him beat himself up when it wasn't his fault. I finally told him if he apologized to me one more time I was gone, but if he could hold his head up and go to work, I would be right there beside him, every step of the way.

"He left for a weekend, and I was really worried that he might harm himself. But he called me on a Saturday night and said he had borrowed enough to buy a yearling that really impressed him and asked me to bring the horse trailer. It's been great ever since."

And here I was—the great friend who didn't know anything about Dale and Sally's struggles. I looked away as I started the truck.

"I didn't tell you about Dale to make you feel guilty. I didn't know about Jim's death. We're both in different lives, wrapped up in our families. People lose touch. But I'm so glad to see you now. And I think we'd better get back to Simon before he finds a cute groom. There's a girl in the barn beside us who wears the tightest jeans. I find Bart brushing a horse, but the brush isn't even touching the horse when she walks by."

"He's a neat kid. Does he want to go into racing?"

"Oh, yeah. He doesn't think he needs to go to school when Keeneland is running. We had to have a few discussions. But he knows he has to finish school first and have a degree of some kind in case the racing goes south."

Sally changed the subject. "What about Will? Why is someone after him, and how did you and Simon get involved?"

"It's Simon's case, and I don't know all the details. And I shouldn't really share what I do know." I eased to a stop in front of their barn.

"It's the details with Simon that I want to know, anyway. What a man to have chasing after you. You'll work it out. I have faith. But you must keep in touch, and I will, too. I have your phone number. I was at your first wedding, and I want to be at the next."

Sally gave me a hug and slid out of the truck. Will ducked out of the tack room and jumped into the back seat, slouching down. Simon climbed in beside me.

"Where to, and what's happening?" I asked him.

"Let's take Will back to the show, and then I need to talk with De Wet. Looks like the Feds got the guy with the stones and one of the golf cart duo. The driver got away. I have to debrief with them tonight."

When we drove up to the barn, grooms and trainers were busy getting ready for the evening's performance. Will disappeared into Rooibos' stall, and I knew that was the best place for him. I offered to hold horses while the grooms finished braiding manes and setting out tack.

Simon took De Wet outside, and they spent a few minutes in deep conversation.

This case reminded me of reading *The Magus*. Reality kept changing.

SEVEN

SIMON WALKED BACK into the barn. "How tired are you?"

"Not bad. What do you have in mind?" The look on his face was serious. I knew this was not a prelude to some fun activity.

"De Wet has a customer near Danville with some extra stalls. Quiet place out in the country. We thought it might be good to take Rooibos and Will. There's a barn apartment where he can stay for a few weeks. Do you feel like you could drive down there with Will and the horse? You can use De Wet's truck and two-horse trailer."

I remembered how Rooibos exited the commercial van. "Okay by me, but how will the stallion feel about it?"

Simon snorted. "We can ask him. More to the point, we can sedate him. I'd go with you, but I still need to debrief tonight."

"What time, Commander?"

"Late-ish, I'm thinking. Maybe leave around nine."

"Buy me dinner and I'm good to go. Mainly caffeine. But what about returning the fake diamonds? I'm responsible for them."

"The FBI has them and will for some time. I told them where they came from, and they promised to return them when they were finished. You can call the professor and tell him."

We found Will and told him the plan. He thought a few weeks out of sight would be great. Simon went to his meeting, and I loaded the trailer according to Will's instructions. He didn't need to aggravate his shoulder any more.

I gave the horse a shot of Acepromazine while Will held him, and we waited for the sedative to take effect. Rooibos walked quietly into the trailer and slowly began munching hay. I closed the tailgate, grabbed a Diet Coke for the trip, and we were off.

As soon as we left Lexington behind, traffic thinned out. I concentrated on the gently winding road. Our destination was about an hour away. Will fell asleep, drained from another scare.

Thirty minutes later I saw the first turn and down-shifted. Will woke, and I handed him the directions. We took two more turns, and I slowed to read a mailbox number. We bumped across the cattle guard and came to a stop in front of a small barn. The security light gave us plenty of vision for unloading. A dog barked nearby. I spotted the house just downhill. A truck started and slowly drove up the hill to the barn.

A tall, slender man, probably in his seventies, stepped out to greet us. "Ms. Jones and Will, welcome. I just have a few old mares left around here, so you'll stir up some excitement sure enough. I'm Bob Young,"

"Mr. Young, we really appreciate this."

I was planning to say more, but Rooibos had awakened and was screaming and pawing, having heard the mares whinny.

"I'd best get him off," Will said as he grabbed the lead line.

Bob turned on the barn lights and opened the door to a freshly bedded double stall.

With a few stern words and a jerk of the lead, Will led the prancing stallion into the stall. Bob insisted on unloading the trailer and then showed Will to the barn office/apartment.

"It's after ten o'clock, Ms. Jones. We have a spare bedroom at the house if you'd like to spend the night."

"I'm good. I'd better head back, but I will use your restroom."

Will watched the stallion to be sure he was settling in. I carried Will's gear to the barn apartment. An office with a futon connected a small kitchenette and an adjoining bath. He would be fine here.

I shook Bob's hand before climbing back into my truck, waved to Will, and started the diesel while I was still wide awake and pumped.

About halfway back to Lexington I got really sleepy, but I cranked up the radio and opened the window. The exit for the motel came none too soon. I hoped there was a parking space big enough for this rig. When I approached the motel, I saw an office building next door. I could leave it there.

I grabbed my purse and jacket and walked wearily toward the motel room. Simon was still awake and immediately enfolded me in a big hug, followed by a kiss.

"Thanks for doing that. I know you've got to be knackered. A drink?"

A drink sounded heavenly. He had a bottle of bourbon and ice. He brought out some cheese from the hotel fridge and a box of crackers. I sat on the bed and took off my boots.

"Will's safe for the moment. Bob Young seems a good man, and he's way out in the boonies. I think he was excited to have a nice horse there. Said they could stay indefinitely."

"De Wet said that Mr. Young would be happy to have guests."

"How was your briefing?"

"Mostly long. But I'll tell you about it tomorrow. Now you need to relax and get some sleep."

He moved behind me and started kneading my shoulders, which were tense from driving the truck and trailer at night on unfamiliar roads. I pulled off my sweater and groaned in pleasure as he continued to massage my back and neck. I sipped my drink and felt myself fading. Simon moved beside me for a kiss.

“Let’s go to sleep, luv. We can lie in a bit in the morning.”

I groggily grabbed my nightshirt and went to brush my teeth. Simon was in bed when I returned. We spooned together, and I was in dreamland.

I thought I had only been asleep a little while when I heard Simon answer his phone. But daylight peeked through the curtains.

“Your son? How long has he been missing? Have you contacted the police?”

Simon’s part of the conversation jolted me awake. *I’d better make some coffee.*

EIGHT

I OVERHEARD ENOUGH of the conversation to know that it was Lord Monkton's son who had disappeared from a townhouse in Alexandria, Virginia. There would be no going back to bed. I dressed and began organizing my scattered belongings.

Simon hung up. "I'll tell you the story over breakfast." He went to shower and shave.

I finished packing and took my stuff out to the truck. Simon followed with his luggage, and we walked to the breakfast room adjacent to the motel office.

"Roger Monkton works as an American correspondent for various news outlets in his father's network. He lives with his partner in a house in Old Town Alexandria. Monkton's ex-wife has been trying to call her son for two weeks. She hasn't been able to get an answer from Roger's or his partner's phones. Said she knew something was bothering Roger last time they talked."

I grabbed some juice and a bagel. "Had Monkton talked to him lately?"

"A few weeks ago. Roger told his dad that he and his partner were having a rough patch, but that's all he would say. He put off some stories he was working on. Monkton's ex wanted to call the police, but he told her to wait until he checked things out. He has a key to their townhouse and is flying to D.C. this morning. Wants us to go with him. You can go home or come along. What do you think?"

I didn't want to leave Simon. "I'm in."

We drove to the airport and put the truck in long-term parking. I'd never flown in a private jet, but I didn't mind learning how the other half lived. We were airborne within twenty minutes.

A middle-aged woman served as the flight attendant. She poured us coffees and offered pastries.

Monkton settled in a chair. "I found out Roger was gay when he was in high school. I had already suspected it. When I became certain, I was distressed, because I knew that life would be more difficult for him, but I've always loved him and tried to accept him for who he was. His friend is a nice enough boy, but weak—not stable financially. I was afraid it would lead to trouble."

Simon turned on his laptop. "What's his partner's name? Does he work?"

"Brian Eddings, an MIT grad. He's very talented with computers. Does contract jobs. He helped research some of Roger's stories. I'm not sure Brian's methods were always aboveboard. I think it was beginning to bother Roger."

Simon worked for a few minutes on his tablet and pulled up a picture. "Is this he?"

Monkton leaned over to look as Simon turned the tablet around. "Yes, that's a fair enough likeness. Does it say anything about him? I know you have sources that I can't tap."

Simon searched a few minutes longer before answering. "He resigned from a bank job a few years ago after the bank discovered a data breach, but he was never charged."

Monkton excused himself to move to his inflight desk and computer.

Simon used the remaining time to search for information about

Roger. He shared a few articles with me. Roger had written guest stories for the Washington Post as well as many for his father's various online and print publications. He seemed to be a man on the way up.

We landed at National where Monkton had hired a car and driver. It was midmorning and raining when we parked outside an attractive brick townhouse. Several days' worth of newspapers littered the small porch.

When Monkton opened the door, Simon insisted on entering first. He asked for the alarm code but when he went to punch it in, he stopped. "It's not activated." Despite the cool, damp day, the air conditioning was running at full force. "Wait here, sir, allow me to check things out."

We stood huddled in the chilly foyer. Simon pulled on gloves as he walked away from us. Monkton shuddered.

The foyer and the adjoining living room were decorated in a comfortable but classic masculine style with lots of leather furniture and a variety of nautical paintings and prints. The room looked lived in and comfortable, a few magazines tossed on the coffee table.

Simon found the thermostat, cut off the air conditioning, and headed upstairs. I jumped as metal crashed and Simon uttered a muted exclamation. "Are you all right?" I yelled.

Simon appeared at the top of the steps. "I am, but someone else is definitely not."

Monkton paled and started toward the stairs. "Has something happened to Roger?"

"Lord Monkton, I don't know, but you need to stay there. This is a crime scene. I'm calling the police." Simon came down the steps.

He handed me a pair of latex gloves. "Put these on and get Sir Monkton a glass of water."

"I need to see, I need to go up there, I need..."

"No, sir," Simon said gently. "We need to stay right here until the police arrive." He led him to a chair in the hall.

Now that the air was turned off I could smell something horrible and dead, but I wondered how much was due to my imagination.

Simon squatted to be at eye level with Monkton. "There is a body upstairs, but it has been there for a while. I don't believe it is your son, but I can't be sure. This is a crime scene and we can't go around mucking it up."

Monkton covered his face with his hands. "I knew something was wrong, I should have asked more, I should have come sooner."

"You don't know that being here would have helped," I said.

I opened the door when I heard sirens in the distance. Simon walked out beside me. "Are you okay, Maddie?"

"Yes, but why can't you tell if it's Roger?" I whispered.

"Later."

A patrolman was first on the scene. He pulled out his radio as he walked upstairs with Simon. A plainclothes officer, who introduced himself as Detective Byrd, came to the door a few minutes later. I directed him upstairs.

Radio chatter and additional sirens filled the air as Monkton pulled out a handkerchief, wiped his face, and took a deep breath. He sat back in the chair, clasped his hands tightly but otherwise tried to appear composed.

I didn't have the words to comfort him, so I concentrated on the room around me. After inspecting the kitchen, Detective Byrd asked us to remain in the foyer and called us one at a time to the kitchen, Simon first. Byrd called him Commander, so I knew Simon had shared his creds. Monkton was next.

Simon and I stepped out on the porch, promising to go no farther until released.

"Why couldn't you tell…"

"The body was beginning to decompose. It had been dismembered and stuffed into a metal garbage can."

I gasped in horror. "Cut apart? Who could do that?"

"A pro could, but why would they? The head is there, so dental records will lead to the identity. Perhaps it's meant to lead us to believe it a rage killing, a falling out of lovers. And it might be that, but I don't think so."

"Because?"

"Because coincidence is all too rare. If Brian was a hacker and Sir Monkton runs a communications empire, there are already too many coincidences. I think Brian was the likely target, and I think the body in the can is too large to have been Roger. But I could be wrong."

My interview was brief. I was asked to tell my version of when we arrived and what happened after that.

Byrd brushed a hand through medium length gray hair and removed his glasses to polish them. He had already recorded our contact information and asked us to remain in town until we heard from him. He offered a ride to our hotel, but Monkton assured him we had a driver waiting. Byrd went out to speak briefly with the driver then released us to go to the hotel.

Monkton insisted on checking us in and assured us that he was covering all expenses. We followed the bellman to his room, and I asked if I could make him a drink from the mini-bar. He nodded.

"Scotch. Straight up. Please. Then you can go on. I've got to call Grace. You've been wonderful. Thank you for coming."

We quietly adjourned to our own room. I chose bourbon and Simon scotch. I had kept the horror at bay, but now I was shaking as I sat down on the couch.

Simon sat beside me and pulled me to him in a hug. "I'm so sorry you had to go through all that. It's the part of my life I want to shield you from."

"But you can't. Not if I am a part of your life too. And I want to be."

"And you are. God help me, you are."

We sat quietly for a few minutes. I snuggled against him, still shivering. Simon got up and found a blanket. He tucked it around me and kissed my forehead before turning on the television to give us some diversion. Picking up the room service menu, he said, "I know you don't feel like eating, but food will help."

"Where is Joe with his magnificent omelets when we need him?" I smiled slightly.

"I suspect they do a fair job here. What strikes your fancy?"

As I read the menu, my stomach rumbled. I was hungry, almost faint from hunger. I opted for grease and protein—a steak sandwich and fries.

Simon ordered and walked to the desk to boot up his tablet. I took a hot shower and pulled on warm sweats while we waited for the food. Simon was on the phone when I came out.

"That's good news, sir. At least you know he's alive. Did she have any idea where he might be?"

I didn't learn anything else from the rest of the conversation. Room service arrived, and I signed for our meal while Simon finished talking.

"Roger called his mother, yesterday, so he's not the victim. He discovered Brian's body, and he's on the run."

NINE

ROGER HADN'T TOLD his mother where he was; only that he was safe and Brian was dead. He had run when he found Brian's body, assuming he would be next.

Monkton remembered that Roger frequently visited Miami. He had a friend, John Ritter, who was a chef in the area. Research showed his friend was still employed at the Royal Sonesta on Key Biscayne, a short drive from Miami.

Once again we were boarding Monkton's private plane. I could get used to this. We deplaned into a humid eighty degrees. The hotel had a vacancy of one of their rental houses, and we knew that would give us more privacy than a room if we did locate Roger. Simon had asked for a rental car rather than a hired driver to give us a lower profile.

I wasn't jet lagged, we hadn't changed time zones, but seeing palm trees complete with iguanas seemed a bit surreal after the crisp fall in Kentucky and rainy cold of northern Virginia. Our three bedroom cottage came complete with its own pool, and I had thrown a bathing suit in my suitcase at the last moment, hoping the Kentucky hotel might have an indoor pool. I swam while Monkton and Simon plotted their approach.

Simon had left without alerting any law enforcement because he wanted to talk to Roger before the FBI got involved or Roger went on the run again.

"Good swim?" Simon asked as he followed me back to our bedroom and bath.

"Heavenly. I'll be dressed in a few minutes. What's the plan?"

"We've located John's house, and I think Monkton has the best shot of making the initial contact if Roger's there. You and I are going biking so dress accordingly."

I had packed for fall in Kentucky, not the tropics, but I threw on a pair of jeans and a t-shirt. I shoved my damp hair under a ball cap. We checked out bikes from the hotel, and Simon pedaled ahead. Our plan was to bike near John's house while Monkton drove over.

The exercise felt good, and I enjoyed seeing the pastel houses with their tropical landscaping. We passed John's two story bungalow and kept going. An ancient Jeep sat in the drive. We circled a cul-de-sac and headed back out to the main drive. The next street should run parallel. We located the property directly behind John's house. A huge mansion was under construction, but there were no workers in sight. Simon texted Monkton that we would soon be in the backyard.

We wheeled our bikes to the back of the lot. A thick, tropical hedge grew behind piles of construction rubble. Trying not to think about snakes, scorpions, and other nasty local wildlife, I followed Simon as he climbed through the brush. We crouched behind some kind of low palm. John's two-story house had a long, screened porch running across the top floor. Steps descended to a small patio. A car, which should be Monkton, pulled onto the crushed shell drive. We heard the peal of the doorbell through the open windows.

A few minutes later, a slim young man ran down the steps from the porch and around toward the front. Simon took off after him, with me in pursuit.

Roger stopped for a moment at the Jeep before he realized it was totally blocked in. Simon used that moment to tackle him and they both rolled to the ground. "Roger, stop."

Roger hesitated for a moment.

"Your father and I are here to help you."

Roger stopped struggling for a moment while he processed the information. "Dad's here?"

"He's at your front door. Will you talk to us?"

Lord Monkton turned when he heard Simon's voice. "Roger, let us help you for God's sake. You're in over your head."

Roger's body went limp. Simon kept his hand on Roger's arm and helped him up. "Let's go inside before the neighbors get curious."

Someone was watching from the door. "Come in, Mr. Monkton. I'm John. Roger talks about you often."

Roger looked sheepishly at his dad as he walked into the house. "I'm sorry."

"Things happen. We need to figure out where to go from here. Take your time and tell us everything."

John offered coffee, and I followed him to the kitchen to help while Simon introduced himself.

When we came back Roger was slumped on a chair with his head in his hands. He took a deep breath and sat back. "I found him. I came in from an hour of running and called out to him. We had argued before I left. I thought he'd gone out, I came upstairs to change and—" Sobs wracked his slender body. "Oh, my God. I knew he was in trouble, but I didn't know it was that bad. I—I—"

Monkton looked at us. Simon spoke. "Let's start at the beginning, shall we?"

"It started about a year ago, I think. Brian was making good money on consulting projects, and I had sold some stories, but he got carried away. He'd never really had any money before.

He began buying expensive clothes, wanted us to go to trendy restaurants. Said he had a new client and things would only be getting better.

"When I tried to tone him down a bit, he said I didn't understand, that I'd been born with a silver spoon. He helped me, too. Gave me some story leads, things I couldn't have known, but he wouldn't tell me how he learned them."

"Government related?" Simon asked.

"Sometimes. Everything in DC connects to government at some level, or private contractors who work with government. Then one night about a month or so ago he began asking me questions about your businesses. About how you got started, what you owned in South Africa.

"At first I was pleased, thought of it as him wanting to know more about you, family history like. But when the questions got more specific, he couldn't meet my eyes. Got very defensive. He'd hardly speak to me, but then he'd try to fix things by giving me a story lead or suggesting we go out for a fun evening. But he was more on edge all the time."

Monkton sighed. "I wish you would have told me."

"I know you never approved of him. I didn't understand what was going on with him, but I still loved him. I didn't comprehend what he'd done, I still don't, not really. But last week, he—he came to me and said he had done something he regretted. Was going to put an end to it."

"Do you know anything about his contacts? Who might have been putting pressure on him?"

"No. He said he couldn't tell me. That he could handle it, and I had to trust him to fix it. And they killed him."

Simon gave Roger a few minutes. The rest of us looked around the room, anywhere except at Roger, who was again sobbing.

Finally, Simon asked, "When did you find him?"

Roger thought a minute. "It was about nine, last Monday night.

I hadn't just gone for a run. I was still upset, so I stopped at a pub, had a few beers, and then decided to go home."

"What did you do when you found him?"

"I was in shock. Who could—I started to call 911 then realized I'd be the chief suspect or else I'd be next. I looked for his computer and his phone and tablet. They were all gone. I grabbed my passport and all the cash I had and took a bus south."

Lord Monkton walked over to his son and put his hand gently on Roger's shoulder. "I've got an attorney lined up. You know we have to go back. You can't run from this."

Roger nodded. "I'll get my things."

I could see a resemblance to his father then, a strength of resolve and a similarity in the way he rose from a chair. I liked him and I believed him. I wondered if Simon did. And I wondered if Simon was beginning to see the whole picture. I sure as hell wasn't.

"See you at the hotel. Thanks for the coffee, John," Simon added.

John hadn't said a word until now. "He needed help. But I didn't know how to help him or what to tell him to do. I'm so glad you came." He looked around. "Did you all come in one car?"

"Simon and I are on bikes," I said. "We parked at the house behind you."

John smiled. "The McMansion to be? I scope it out every week just to see how the other half plans to live." He looked at Monkton and a blush began to creep up his face. "I mean how they build, I mean..."

Monkton smiled for the first time that day. "Your home is very welcoming, John. Thanks for taking Roger in."

We scooted through the brush and found our bikes. Simon smiled at me. "Let's be off then."

I spent the ride back wondering what he was thinking.

Roger and his dad spent some time reconnecting before Simon resumed grilling him in private.

I was so confused. Who smuggled the diamonds? Who ended

up with them and why? How was this connected to Brian's murder, and what was the final goal? If we started at the end, it would seem Brian was murdered because he no longer was willing to hack into whatever he was hacking. And since all the events were swirling around Lord Monkton, he was either the target or the means to the target. Simon knew more, of course, since he was tipped off about the smuggling in the beginning, but I was pretty sure he wasn't too far ahead of me as to the entire picture.

I wanted to ask Simon for a flow chart. I flopped on the bed and turned on the TV, and the next thing I knew, it was dark outside and Simon was asking me if I wanted dinner. Once I woke up enough to understand where I was, we walked over to the hotel. Lord Monkton and Roger were ordering room service.

"We're flying back to Virginia in the morning," Simon told me.

"What will happen with Roger?"

"I've already spoken to Lt. Byrd. Roger will turn himself in as a material witness. His attorney will meet him at the police station. Then we'll see where it goes. He understands he will probably have to spend time in jail. The attorney will have a hard time proving that he's not a flight risk."

"For sure."

After an excellent seafood dinner, we walked back to the cottage and I called Dad. He and Joan and the dogs were all fine. I told him where we were and promised details when I returned.

***

The pilot was walking around the plane doing his preflight check when he suddenly stopped and asked for a flashlight. My phone rang.

"Hi, Dad."

"I don't think you want to get on that plane, Maddie, and neither does anyone else."

My father's weird fire sense had saved me more than once, so I was definitely a believer. "Simon, the plane, it's not safe," I said as

I began to back away.

Simon herded Monkton, his flight attendant, and Roger away from the jet and called to the pilot. “There may be a problem, are you seeing something wrong?”

“Maddie?” came my father’s voice.

“Thanks, Dad. I think the pilot spotted something. Later.”

TEN

THE PILOT POINTED toward the wheel well. "I didn't order any servicing except fuel, but the wheel well looks like someone's been there."

An evening shower had blown puddles of rain on the tarmac, and the remains of wet footprints went toward the undercarriage of the plane.

Simon yelled, "Stand back, I think we need a bomb squad."

The pilot turned to Monkton. "I'd do as he says."

Simon looked at me. "Get Roger out of sight while we handle this."

Roger glanced from his father to Simon, sweating and antsy. "What's the matter?"

I took his arm. "Come with me. You don't want to be telling the local police who you are."

Monkton gave us his VIP pass so that we could return to the private air terminal. We watched a canine unit pull onto the field and additional bomb experts piled from the terminal. The squad worked under the plane for over twenty minutes while Simon and Monkton paced. The officers brought something out and showed it to Monkton and Simon before continuing their search.

"How did you know?" Roger asked.

I told him about my dad and his strange ESP.

"Do you have it too?"

"Maybe a little. Until last year I would have said no, but maybe I always had it, just didn't need it. But I'm not as sensitive as my father."

Roger alternated between looking out the window and pacing the room. He poured himself a cup of coffee and offered me one.

"Sure, thanks. How are you doing? I know the last few days have been hell for you."

He turned to face me. "Yeah. I made everything worse by running. And to think my dad had to walk in and find Brian, maybe even think it was me. I never meant for that to happen. I never wanted to cause him grief, only for him to be proud of me. He—he's always stood up for me, you know. Allowed me to follow my own path, more than Mom did really.

"He was right about Brian, but I couldn't see it. And even when I did, God help me, I still loved him. Can you even understand that?" He handed me my coffee.

I wasn't sure what he was really asking. Did he mean his loving a man in general or loving a man with problems? I forged ahead. "Roger, we can't help whom we fall in love with, we can only make choices knowing whatever we know and trying to be realistic about the consequences."

"You and Simon are together, right? I mean not just work partners?"

Oh, boy. "Simon helped me track down what happened to my husband in Afghanistan. I learned the truth and despite my grief over Jim and despite our resolve, we did fall in love."

Now it was my turn to walk around the room, to think about what I wanted to say. Roger was too sensitive to accept vague platitudes. "We both felt guilty and afraid, but in the end, love happens, and you have to choose whether it is worth pursuing. I was numb for a long time after Jim died and when I got caught up in the adventure, I felt guilty for living again. Then I realized that if what Jim and I had was real and good, he would want me to find it again—not to spend my life in a shell. But Simon and I haven't exactly worked everything out, yet."

My phone buzzed when Simon's text came. "Monkton's leased another plane, should be ready in about thirty minutes."

Simon met us on the way. "The bomb squad pulled a small explosive out of the wheel well. It was fairly obvious. I suspect it was meant more to scare us than to harm us. But good that we found it. Call your dad back."

"Dad, there was a small bomb. They thoroughly searched the plane—but we're leasing another. How's your hunch machine?"

"I don't predict storms, turbulence, or low flying geese. But I feel okay now. Be safe, Maddie."

"Will do. Love you and thanks."

Simon watched me as I put away my phone. "Good?"

"Good."

We were quiet until after takeoff. When we settled at flying altitude, I leaned over to Simon. "So who was the target, and who knows where we are?"

"I'm guessing someone's watching Monkton's comings and goings. His pilot had to file a flight plan."

"Will the cops meet us at the airport?"

"No. I didn't elaborate as to how we were coming, only that we would be there this morning. I've alerted the attorney about the delay."

Roger slept. I doubted if he'd been sleeping lately, and things were going to be worse for him before they got any better. Monkton planned to move into Roger's house since it was no longer a crime scene. He invited us to join him, but Simon said he wasn't sure where he needed to be.

Simon rented a car at the airport and we followed the Monktons to the Alexandria Police Station. Simon went in to meet the attorney and then brought him out to meet Roger. I sat in the rental and checked my email.

Human Services had scheduled a meeting about my foster daughter-to-be. In spite of the bad press that social workers received, I had been impressed with their due diligence. In addition to training classes, a home inspection, references, various certifications, and a background check, they had required a test of my well water. Everything passed and the social worker was ready to meet with me prior to a placement hearing. I had waited months for this, but the timing sucked.

Simon came out alone. "I think we've done all we can for Roger and his father here. I need to solve the case to really help them."

"So where are you off to?"

"Not including yourself in my plans?"

"I don't know. I want to go with you if you'll have me, but DSS waits in Charleston."

"Good news?"

"I think so." Simon was all in favor of me, and eventually us, fostering and maybe adopting one of the Turkmen girls we had rescued. But our future timetable hadn't exactly been discussed.

"Then you need to take care of that. But first let's go to Charleston, visit your dad. And see your house. I've got to research a few things before I go back. Today's Tuesday. Let's catch a flight tomorrow, and I can stay until Sunday if nothing else goes south."

We found a hotel near the airport, and Simon spent the rest of the day on his tablet and phone. I scheduled the DSS meeting, and Simon scheduled a meeting with his Charleston FBI connections.

At seven he powered off his device and put his arm around my shoulder. "Let's go find a drink and dinner, shall we? Work can wait."

We went to the hotel pub and ordered wine. Simon was quiet until our glasses arrived. "Sla'inte, Maddie."

We toasted and sipped. "Maddie, I'm sorry we've not had more time for us. This case has become more complicated by the minute. But seeing you, having you with me, makes me know I need to make some changes soon. I'm not ready to retire, exactly, but I'm looking into other options."

"Like?"

"I'm not sure, but you realize that I don't only work for the Garda. My liaisons have been more European, but they could become more American allowing me to be here a good part of the year. That is, assuming you'd want me around?"

"Simon. You needn't ask. And if this fostering leads to adoption, I wouldn't mind living in Ireland."

"Everyone wants to live in Ireland. It's not me; it's my bloody country you're after."

I laughed. "Yes, all I want is a green card or whatever they're called in Ireland. Surely they are green? Actually, I guess Americans can live in Ireland as long as they want to. It's making a living that might be a problem."

"Many of my countrymen have that problem as well since the Celtic Tiger died. But it's getting better. I would be supporting you."

"My truck."

"You want that truck in Ireland?"

"No. We can't fly to Charleston. My truck's still in Lexington."

"Oh. You know, I suspect Sir Monkton's pilot has to fly back and exchange planes anyway. I'm sure he'd be glad to give us a ride to Lexington first."

"Or what about Joe? Is he staying there or coming to meet you? Maybe he could drive it."

"No, actually he's gone home for a bit, family reunion for his father's eightieth birthday."

"Where is his home?"

"He mostly grew up in Trinidad but his father is South African, worked on cargo ships, met Joe's mother in the Caribbean. Joe went to high school and university in South Africa after apartheid ended."

No wonder I couldn't place his accent.

"He's not only going for personal reasons, is he?"

Simon called for the check. "No, but the reunion makes good cover. When it's over, he'll go to Bloemfontein and check on Will's wife."

As Simon had predicted, Monkton's pilot agreed to fly us to Lexington early the next morning. Then we would drive to Charleston. Sally said she would be happy to bring my truck to the airport since they had to be at Keeneland anyway.

I called Dad with the plans.

"I'll be glad to see both of you. Your stepmother has some information for Simon from one of her old contacts. She was going to call, but it might be better in person."

ELEVEN

SIMON HAD BEEN talking seriously about our future, and I had interrupted him with travel details. Where was my head, and why couldn't I learn to keep my mouth shut? Should I mention it or wait for him? Sometimes I felt like a teenager.

Sally and Dale met us at the airport.

"I packed sandwiches and cookies for your drive," Sally said, as she handed me a bag. "I was having a domestic moment." Not only that, but the truck was full of diesel and freshly washed.

"Wow," I said. "I am definitely going to stay in touch."

Sally laughed. "After Bart drove your truck to the back pasture and got stuck in the mud, we had to wash it."

I didn't deserve friends like this. I hadn't made time or space in my life for them, but they remained nonetheless. I vowed to do better as I hugged them goodbye. Simon thanked them as well as we headed south into the frosty morning.

Simon was busy on his phone and tablet while I drove. We stopped for coffee outside of Knoxville and broke out the sandwiches.

"Did your father give you a hint of what your stepmother wanted to tell me?"

"Only that it had to do with a former contact who works for Reuters."

"Monkton seems a decent sort. But he won't have made it to where he is without making enemies along the way. The people who are being threatened or in Brian's case, murdered, are peripheral to Monkton."

"Those around him are being targeted as a means to an end."

"Yes. And I think I might be getting a lead on the end. Maddie, you worked in newspapers. How much checking would you do on a story from a wire service?"

"I'm not the one to ask. I mostly worked for local papers. We didn't use much off the wire services unless it had a local connection. But if it came through as usual, not much unless it was very strange or shocking news. Then someone would double check. Wait—you think that's what Brian was doing? Planting stories? Hacking into the wire services?"

"I think it likely. But I don't know if the object was financial or political gain."

"Or maybe both. One usually leads to the other."

When we stopped for fuel outside Columbia, the temperature was a balmy seventy degrees. "This is why I live in the South."

"I thought you wanted to live in Ireland?"

I grabbed Simon's arms on each side and pulled him to face me. "I want to live where you are."

"And I want you to be my wife. To have a home with you and our adopted daughter. But one thing at a time." He laughed. "Romantic spot for a proposal, isn't it?"

I slid my arms up around his neck and kissed him. Were we not standing in front of a gas pump, we might have been delayed in our travels. I did indeed want to be with Simon, to someday be his wife. But the how and where and when were complicated. Beyond the kiss, I wasn't sure how to answer. I wanted my nest and to be a mother—not biologically, an infant was not in my vision. The

Turkmen girls had touched my soul and I knew I could help at least one. Simon appeared to want an adopted daughter as much as I did. I loved him, but could I make it all work?

***

Katie and Dipsy met us at the condo door. Only after lavishing them with pats, ear rubs, and scratches was I free to hug my dad.

"Come have a drink. Dinner's almost ready."

I could smell something redolent of wine, beef, and garlic. "Let me take Katie for a quick walk, and I'll be ready."

I knew I would have no peace until she and I had some quality time. I grabbed her leash and hit the sidewalk, remembering to stuff a poop bag in my pocket. The Daniel's Island neighborhood was beautifully landscaped with lots of sidewalks and flower beds. After the plane and the drive, I needed the exercise as much as she needed the attention.

I turned her loose in the dog play area and she grabbed an abandoned ball, dropping it at my feet. After several bouts of retrieving I hooked on the leash, and we jogged back to the condo.

Dad poured me a glass of wine and we sat down with Simon and Joan. "Maddie, I'm so happy for you. Simon told me the good news."

"News?" I looked at Simon. "Oh, you mean about my foster daughter."

"Actually I asked for his blessings." Simon had the grace to look sheepish.

Now I was embarrassed. "Oh, well, we haven't made any plans yet."

Dad looked at both of us. "But you will. You will."

"I think it's time to eat." I was not ready to discuss my love life or my concerns until we had worked everything out.

We filled our plates with beef burgundy and homemade garlic bread. Dad blessed the food and poured more wine.

"As I was telling Simon, my friend Rupert told me that his

agency was having trouble with bogus stories coming across. The stories appeared randomly and no one could trace their origin."

Simon thought for a minute. "Can you ask if they were sent to several media outlets or only a few? And if only a few, which ones?"

Joan might be retired, but she was quick. "You're thinking Monkton's media might be targeted? Let's see, Rupert's in Africa now. I'll email him tonight."

We were tired and excused ourselves early. Simon put his arms around me as soon as we closed the door. "Sorry if I embarrassed you. I wanted your father to know my intentions were honorable."

"I didn't know you James Bond types were so old-fashioned. And I haven't answered your proposal yet."

"Maddie, love, I'm not trying to rush you. I have to organize my life differently. I'm working on that, but it will take some time."

I leaned in for a kiss. We didn't sleep for a long time, but then we both fell into deep dreamless rest.

I woke at daylight and turned on the TV to check the weather. National news was showing an assassination attempt in Alexandria. A sniper had taken a shot at Roger as he entered the federal courthouse. Video feed showed him being hustled inside, but he didn't appear to be injured.

I yelled to Simon in the shower. He came out in time to hear a recap. Monkton called before Simon could call him. Simon encouraged him to hire extra security for himself and assured him that law enforcement would be vigilant. Roger was already being held in a private cell due to security risks.

Simon checked in with Alexandria and found out there was no lead on the shooter. The would-be assassin had fired from a passing car. Simon turned on his tablet and read an email from Joe about a bomb threat at one of Monkton's South African media outlets. Apparently no bomb had been found, but a ticking timer had been placed in a main air vent with a warning note.

These villains had long arms in many places.

"Go on down to breakfast, love. I need to make some phone calls, but tell your stepmother I'll be along shortly."

Pans clanged, bacon sizzled and scented the air. Katie was pawing to get out of our closed bedroom door. I found Dad in the kitchen and learned that Joan was walking Dipsy. I grabbed Katie's lead and set out. We caught up in the next block, and I learned the latest from her journalist friend.

"He's made some discreet inquiries. Most of the outlets who received the bogus stories were Monkton's, but not all. And there's a new twist. While some fake stories were sent, other legitimate stories were pulled from certain outlets. It all happened electronically, and no one at Reuters can trace the source."

I told her about Roger's attempted murder.

"My God, these people are everywhere. What do you suppose is their ultimate goal?"

"Simon may have some idea, but I haven't heard it yet."

"We'd better get back before your father has breakfast on the table."

"Yeah, about that. Does he cook often? I'm having trouble with this new image."

She laughed. "We took a cooking class together. I could tell he was a little out of his depth, but he likes cooking breakfast, and I'm fine with it."

Simon pulled me aside when we returned with the dogs. "I've been summoned home. New developments in Ireland. I'm sorry, but I have to fly out tonight."

TWELVE

EVEN THOUGH I had known he was planning to leave soon, the immediacy caught me by surprise. I had been trying not to think about it, to enjoy our time together as it unfolded. My face must have shown my disappointment.

Simon pulled me into a hug. "After breakfast, I want to see your cottage. I don't have to leave until tonight. And, God willing, you can come to Ireland soon if I'm not back."

We broke the news over breakfast and quickly packed our things. I promised to come for dinner again often. Katie was excited to join us in the truck for the drive out to the farm.

Simon commented only on the scenery, so I assumed he couldn't tell me any more about the latest developments.

I drove through the farm gates and turned onto a lane lined with live oaks dripping Spanish moss. Even in the fall their evergreen foliage was lush.

The low country style cottage sat above a small carport and storage area. The steps led to a good sized screened porch, which I had decorated with painted thrift store finds and recovered cushions. A potted palm and a croton added color and life.

Simon inspected my deadbolt after I unlocked the bright peach front door. He stopped at the view in front of him.

"It's lovely, Maddie. You did all of this yourself?"

"I hired a plumber and electrician and then a carpenter to help in the kitchen, but the decor and paint jobs are all mine, along with the refinished floors."

I suddenly felt shy and self-conscious. I was revealing more of myself. My father had given me whatever furniture I wanted from his house when he and Joan were married, and I had enough money when my North Carolina property and burned out house sold to purchase appliances and such. I didn't yet own the cottage, but I had sweat equity and a very reasonable option to buy.

Simon walked around quietly, pausing to study a painting or a piece of furniture. He raised his eyebrows comically when he spotted my queen size bed. The bedroom which I hoped would house my foster daughter was painted the palest of pinks with a black, old-fashioned metal bed. I had decided to wait and allow her to choose her bedcovers and pictures.

We ended up in the kitchen and I made tea.

"I can see why your nest calls to you, Maddie. You really have created a special place here, a haven where you can heal and hide when you need to. But also a place to share your love. I would feel quite comfortable in your cottage—that is, whenever I might be invited."

I reached for his hand. "That would be anytime." I sipped my tea. "And for as long as you wished. But would you give up Ireland?"

"The old sod is only a plane ride away, and who knows how we will work things out? As long as you are in my life, I think I could adjust. When is your meeting with social services?"

"Monday afternoon. I should have an idea about the timetable on foster placement then."

"I'll call you after. I really want you to come to Ireland for Christmas."

We walked across the farm, through pastures full of mares

or weanlings. The owners had several broodmares, mostly Warmbloods, but a few Saddlebreds. They also did foaling out for other owners, and I suspected I would spend many winter evenings in the foaling barn.

Live oaks and pecan trees surrounded the cottage. The afternoon had grown pleasantly warm, and we sat in two old metal chairs I had rescued from a roadside. By unspoken mutual agreement, we hadn't discussed the case. I knew Simon would share what he could, but this time was too precious to squander on anything but us.

I hadn't really answered his proposal. I had an idea. "Simon, why don't we apply for a marriage license before you leave? We could use it anytime when you come back—they don't expire."

He froze. Did he not really mean it? But then he smiled. "Maddy, that's a wonderful idea—so you will have me? How do we do this?"

"The probate office. We can stop on the way to the airport if we leave now."

I invited the dog to go with us so I wouldn't have to come home alone. As usual, she hopped eagerly into the truck. We ran into the office ten minutes before closing and I'm sure annoyed everyone. I didn't care. I could pick up the license the next day and hold it until?

***

Simon worked his phone for a few minutes then turned to me. "I have my boarding pass and a security line bypass so you can just drop me off and not have to leave Katie in the truck. Will should be safe for the moment in Kentucky, and you shouldn't be in any danger. Lord Monkton is going to Ireland, and we will be keeping up with his son's case. But you can call me anytime. If anything seems off around your farm, call your dad. He has a good sense of things."

"In addition to his sixth sense?"

Simon laughed. "You know that punning is the lowest form of

intellectual humor?"

"Better than the maudlin thoughts I'm having." I was trying not to cry as I pulled into the airport departure area. I put the truck in neutral and stamped on the emergency brake.

He reached over and lifted my chin as he leaned toward me. "Be safe, love, and know that I love you."

"Simon, promise me you won't do anything risky."

"Risky is part of the game, but I have more reason to stay in one piece now. But you know all of that. Good luck with Sanda. Maddie, we will make this work." With that he grabbed his luggage and headed for the door.

I wiped my eyes and ground the truck into first gear in response to a honking cab behind me. I did not gesture what I really felt to the vehicle behind me, which should have given me some Heavenly credit.

***

I went to the main barn and helped with afternoon chores, anything to keep busy. The weekend was full of weaning foals and all the watchfulness and noise that involves. We made sure there were no loose boards or other hazards in the weaning stalls. Then we led the mares and foals in and took the mare back out, quickly shutting the stall door between them. We had four babies to wean, and two of the mares were more than done with their babies, two stud colts six months old and very demanding. The fillies were a bit younger and their dams started whinnying as soon as the door closed. One colt started in on his hay with a minimum of fuss, but the others ran the length of their stalls rearing and nickering.

We turned the mares out together, out of sight of the babies. They called once or twice but then went to grazing with only an occasional whinny.

Back in the barn we spoke softly to the weanlings and hoped that none of them would injure themselves in their distress. They had all been eating grain for at least a month, so when they began to settle we gave them their evening feed and filled their water buckets. Gradually, the noise subsided.

Sunday night I was ready for my bed and eager for Monday's meeting when my phone rang.

"Is that Maddie there?"

The call was not, as I had hoped, from Simon. "Who is this?"

THIRTEEN

"IT'S WILL—WITH Rooibos, you know?"

"Yes, Will, of course. How are you? Is everything all right?" I hoped he was calling with an untraceable prepaid cell.

"I'm worried sick, I am. Mr. Young is in the hospital. Had to have heart surgery. I need help."

"Do you need food or horse feed or what?"

"Oh, no. The stud is fine, and I've laid up a bunch of frozen dinners. But my wife sent me a message. She has, we both have, old Facebook accounts. Mr. Young let me use his computer. Anise is pregnant, I didn't know, you see. She wasn't sure until after I left, and she didn't want to worry me. But the stress. The baby's trying to come too early, she's in hospital, and I need to be with her."

The words were pouring out faster than I could process them. "Will, I'm listening, but please slow down."

"Okay, Miss, but I've got no money, and I can't leave this horse without someone who can take care of him. I've tried to call Lord Monkton, but I can't get him. I don't know what to do."

I didn't know what to do either, but I might be able to find him some help. "Will, calm down. Of course you're worried, but give me some time to call a few people. Simon's not here now, but I can call him. Give me your number."

He had called from the Young's landline, which should be safe enough if no one knew where he was and if my phone wasn't bugged. But since I was still using the Blackberry Simon had given me for security purposes, I was probably safe on my end as well.

Simon's phone went immediately to voice mail and again when I tried twenty minutes later. I decided to try De Wet. I looked up his stable on my computer and eventually located a cell number.

"It's Madelaine Jones. We met at the Horse Park, I was with Simon."

De Wet was gracious and asked how he could help me. I told him that Will was going to have to go somewhere and needed a safe place to leave the stallion. I asked if we could bring the stud back to his barn.

"That's a bit of a problem," he said. "I'm actually at a show in St. Louis. I wouldn't be comfortable with anyone else handling him until I get back—I'll be home Tuesday night, could he hold out till then?"

"I guess he'll have to. Can you pick him up or do I need to arrange transport?"

"It would be better if you could bring Will and the horse. My two-horse trailer is with me—I'm going to look at some horses on the way home, won't be back until Tuesday night at the earliest. But you and Will could bring the horse anytime as long as he stays with him."

I tried Simon again to no avail and considered the situation. The attempt on Will's life at the show was a few weeks ago. Will and the horse should be able to stay safe at De Wet's barn now. I didn't think anyone was waiting around to harm him. Dale might be able to haul the horse, but I didn't want to ask for more favors. My trailer was parked behind my house. The simplest thing I could come up with was to go back to Kentucky and pick up Will and the horse after my meeting with social services, on Monday morning.

Will called back before I had a chance to call him. I assured him that I would be there sometime Monday night, but he would have to stay with the horse until De Vet got home. I promised I would find a way to get him a ticket. Surely Monkton would spring for the ticket, but I had no idea how to find him.

I tried Simon one last time and decided to call it a night. But the what if's left me tossing and turning.

Katie whimpered at six, and I got up to let her out, wondering if I had slept at all. I made coffee and took a shower which helped a little. My makeup didn't quite cover the dark circles under my eyes, but at least I was looking a bit more human. Social Services would think I was going to be an unfit parent who cavorted away the night.

I told Jane I was leaving for Kentucky at noon and checked the tires on the trailer. I threw in a water bucket and a bale of hay and hay net as well as my emergency vet kit. Then I added food and a water dish for Katie.

How should I dress for the meeting? Navy slacks and a red sweater looked like a passable choice. After I added a scarf, I decided I looked somewhat presentable. If they were going to turn me down now, it wouldn't matter what I was wearing.

Still no word from Simon. I double checked my messages and texts for the tenth time.

Beth, the social worker assigned to Sanda, welcomed me with a smile. "Come in, Madelaine, I think we mostly need to finish some paperwork."

She shuffled papers while I found a seat. "You passed the home inspection, background check, and everything looks good, but there is one wrinkle."

I tensed. My stomach dropped. Something I had done or left undone? A forgotten incident from my past was going to ruin my reputation? "What's the problem?"

"Sanda has a half-sister, who's in med school at NYU. She didn't know what had happened to her sister, only that she was no longer in Turkmenistan."

"Would she want custody?" My voice wavered. After all of my planning and work to be approved as a foster parent, a sister appears. Where was she when Sanda was wounded by an IED? Where was she when Sanda was kidnapped, raped, and sold into slavery as a nanny? I should be glad for her, but my heart didn't want to give her up.

Beth looked up. "No. At least not now. They've not seen each other since Sanda was a baby. But the sister would like to meet her—she suggested Christmas break with the sister's adoptive family. That's assuming we can get the background checks completed by then."

I had been about to ask if there was any possibility of taking her to Simon's with me for Christmas. "That would be okay with me. I actually have been invited to Ireland for Christmas."

"Lucky you. I'm sure we can arrange respite care one way or another. I'm thinking Sanda would come to you in two weeks, does that work?"

I smiled, relief flooding through me. I was soon to be a foster parent. "Yes, of course."

Feeling upbeat, I sang along with Pink on the radio while I drove back to the farm to load. After changing to jeans, I hitched the trailer and grabbed a Diet Coke and peanut butter and jelly sandwich for the road. Katie jumped in, and we were ready to roll.

The first few hours flew by but then my eyes started drooping. I stopped for diesel, filled up on caffeine, and called my dad.

"Have you heard from Simon?" he asked.

"No. I tried to call him, but so far all I get is voice mail. I sent him a text that I was headed to Kentucky to pick up Will and the stud."

"You sound a bit down, in spite of your good news. Are you feeling all right?"

"Just tired. I didn't sleep too well. But I'm sure I'll be fine." I didn't tell him I was beginning to feel distinctly unwell.

"Will can wait another day if you need to stop somewhere. No sense driving if you're too tired."

"I'll call you if I stop. Bye, Dad."

Was I coming down with something? I didn't think I had a fever. I didn't ache. My throat wasn't sore. I tried to analyze how I was feeling. Dread. That's what I felt. Surely I wasn't having a heart attack. I saw a rest area ahead and pulled in.

Was this a premonition? Should I stop now, sleep in the truck? Simon filled my mind—maybe my subconscious was reacting to my worry. I started to call Dad, but the feeling grew worse. I knew it was Simon, and I knew he was in danger—I didn't see flames just a wall of darkness. I grabbed the phone and texted, "Danger—you!"

FOURTEEN

KATIE WHINED, NO doubt a reaction to my panic and resulting surge of adrenalin. I searched for a news station on the radio, and I called my father to tell him what was happening.

"I didn't really see anything but darkness. I knew it concerned Simon, like last fall when I could tell you were in danger and that hunter almost shot you."

"That's why you sounded so odd. I knew something was wrong, and this explains it. How do you feel now?"

"Scared and worried and totally drained. But I don't feel sick anymore. Is this how a premonition is for you? Why didn't I have any of these reactions when Jim was in danger?" I sobbed out the last words, "Didn't I love him enough?"

"Maddie, Maddie, you can't control premonitions any more than you can control the weather. I never had any when your mother got sick, only about fires and explosions. Heed them when they happen, but there is nothing for you to feel guilty about. Your love or connection to a person doesn't guarantee a warning. I count them a blessing when they help, like when your house burned..."

"Got to go, message on my phone."

"You were right, but okay now, call later," appeared on my screen.

Thank God. I was spent and shaking. I had never eaten my sandwich, so I gobbled down the peanut butter and jelly. The sugar helped. I went to the concession area, bought a bottle of water, and took Katie for a walk. The map showed I was close to Knoxville, so I could find a motel there. I called Dad back while I searched for a place to stay. Will would have to wait.

The Motel 6 looked clean and well kept. I found a spot big enough for the truck and trailer. After calling Will and ignoring his protests about my delay, I fed the dog and took a shower.

The phone chimed when I was almost asleep. "Maddie, I'm sorry I couldn't get back to you earlier. What's going on with Will?"

"Simon, are you really okay? I had a vision or a feeling or something. It was awful. I... I thought you would die."

"There was a bit of a dust-up. We learned from an informer that another of Lord Monkton's properties was targeted, a TV station this time. I was inside trying to insist the manager evacuate the employees when I received your text. I pulled the fire alarm and shouted for everyone to run. We all got out before the bomb went off. Thank God. Impeccable timing, luv."

I was speechless. I knew what he did for a living, but would I always be terrified of losing him? I had taken the risk to love again, but could I handle the danger?

"Maddie?"

I took a deep breath and tried to get my emotions under control. "Simon, I was so terrified, and now I feel totally wiped out."

"Tell me about Will. And how did your meeting with Social Services go?"

The change of subject was abrupt, but Simon knew what he was doing. I focused on answering the questions and calmed down. I explained everything and yawned through the last few sentences. Simon said, "I want you to sleep till noon and Will be damned along with the horse he rode in on."

I laughed and said good night

Katie and I were on the road by seven and made it to Will around nine-thirty. He had everything packed up and had already worked Rooibos to take the edge off. I gave the horse a shot of Ace and waited a few minutes for the tranquilizer to take effect.

Will paced the barn aisle as if he could hurry the drug along.

"Simon will get you a ticket to South Africa. He'll call me back with the details. Have you heard any more from your wife? Is she having premature contractions?"

"I told her I would call as soon as I knew something. She said she was stable for now, the contractions have stopped."

Had Joe's family reunion in South Africa ended? Was he still in the country? If so, he could keep an eye on Will and his wife.

We loaded up and Rooibos walked agreeably onto the trailer. I remembered to call De Wet's caretaker to let him know we were on the way. He said he had a stall bedded and ready. The trainer should be home that evening.

We made the trip to Simpsonville in an hour, with Rooibos pawing and kicking around every turn. Guess I should have given him a higher dose.

"He's a right terror to haul," Will said, glancing back toward the trailer. "I had to really knock him out for the flights. But I think De Wet can handle him; he's seen enough of how he acts. I've been in such a state, I never thanked you. I know you didn't have to come get me. I was so panicked about Elsa and the horse and everything, I wasn't thinking about anybody else."

"I know you've been through a lot. How's your shoulder?"

"I'd say, 'Right as rain,' but that's when I feel the bloody thing. But I'm almost back to normal."

Will jumped out before I stopped the rig. He unloaded the horse while I checked my messages. Simon had arranged for a ticket out of Louisville leaving Wednesday night.

De Wet's caretaker told Will he could bunk in the lounge. Knowing we had a plan, he relaxed enough to stand still while I gave him the details about his flight. He started to say goodbye with a handshake that morphed into an awkward hug. Then he headed off to help the caretaker work the remaining horses and finish barn chores.

I turned my rig around and headed for the highway home. Premonitions, parenthood, and the convoluted case whorled in my thoughts. I turned on the radio and tried to keep my mind on the road.

The "Why Monkton?" question kept popping up. I understood that media manipulation could result in financial gain or political capital, but why was he specifically targeted? The recruitment of his son's lover and framing of Roger for the murder were very personal. Simon might know. But, if so, he hadn't shared the reason with me.

I knew the Garda would be looking into Monkton's business rivals and searching for other enemies. In a business empire as large as his, the possibilities were huge. Former employees, partners, suppliers could all be involved.

But I kept thinking about the personal nature of the attacks. An idea struck me. I remembered a case from my newspaper days. Right before I had gone to work for a small weekly paper, a woman had sent in a birth announcement. The editor printed it without giving a second thought. Trouble was, it was bogus. And the same edition carried the wedding announcement of the supposed father to a local girl.

The groom-to-be was a psychologist and one of his deluded patients had fantasized a romantic relationship. She posted the announcement in hopes of breaking up the engaged couple. Lawsuits loomed, but fortunately the bride had enough faith in her fiancée to believe him. The wedding took place as planned, and the disturbed woman was eventually arrested for stalking the wife and trying to hire a hitman.

What if one of Monkton's papers had printed a similar untruth, and the results were devastating to someone? I think it would have had to happen early on when he had more personal and less corporate responsibility. I wondered if he had ever worked as an editor.

FIFTEEN

I USED MY last ounce of concentration to pull in the driveway. I lingered outside long enough for Katie to do her business before I hit the shower and bed.

I rejoined the world the next morning by email. I had a long note from Katerina in Ireland saying that one of her customers in America wanted to retire his Akhal-Teke. He would lease the mare for free to anyone who would breed her as long as he had an option to buy the foal. Best of all, he was in favor of cross breeding, possibly to a Saddlebred. Jane had one older Saddlebred stallion with decent bloodlines and a great temperament. I had enjoyed working with his babies. And I was certainly interested in seeing how a Saddlebred-Teke cross might turn out.

I emailed her confirming my interest. She would get back to me after she talked to the mare owner.

There was no word from Social Services, which I took as good news. I couldn't help but think about the murder and the diamonds. I wondered what Simon knew that I didn't.

I hoped Roger Monkton would be exonerated. I was pretty sure he hadn't murdered his lover. Jail was the safest place for him now but I wondered, given the reach of these criminals, if it were safe enough.

And what about Simon? Could I handle the fact that he was often in danger? Did having premonitions make it better? Or worse? I was thoroughly muddled and decided to go to the barn. I worked the young horse which had been my project and mentioned to Jane the possibility of breeding an Akhal-Teke mare to her stallion. She was all in favor and said I wouldn't even need to pay a breeding fee. I could trade out for work.

When I walked back to the cottage for lunch, I unhitched my trailer and cleaned out Rooibos's leavings. Will really did owe me. I had a thought. Were they breeding Rooibos yet? If I got my mare, would he give me a stud fee? Jane's stallion was okay, but nothing like the South African horse. Visions of a metallic coated foal reaching for the sky filled my mind. I was so engrossed in my daydreaming that I didn't hear my phone ringing until the last peal.

"Hey, Simon. I'm home and rested. How about you?"

Simon gave a few more details of his "dust-up," and I remembered to ask him about Monkton. "Did he ever work as an editor or reporter for a small paper? Everything seems so personal that I was thinking maybe the root of all this could go way back."

Simon didn't know, but he would add that to his list of questions when he met with Monkton the next day.

A list of questions seemed like a good idea. I opened a Diet Coke and sat down at my kitchen table. There was so much going on in my life, and I needed to first sort it by categories before I even knew the next step. I started with Sanda. Under her name I wrote: When? What? Still needed? Sister? Medical care?

Sanda had a bad limp from an IED explosion near her home. The injury was never properly treated, but DSS planned to have her leg evaluated to see if anything could be done. She also had a prominent facial scar, and I was pretty sure it could be helped by plastic surgery. Would DSS or Medicaid be willing to pay for that?

Not to mention counseling. I knew she would need that as well. Assuming I was able to adopt her, I would need to find a full-time job with benefits.

The next column was a list of my questions about Monkton's case: Who gave Will the diamonds, who ended up with them, why Monkton, why Will, what was the goal?

I didn't try to answer any questions, only listed them. I labeled the next group Simon. Danger? Christmas? Marriage? Where to live? Was I ready? And then there was Sanda. Simon had assured me last summer that he wanted us to adopt one of the Turkmen orphans, but how did that work into the whole marriage scenario?

Monkton's case was the least emotionally disturbing to me, so I decided to concentrate on that, after I heard back from Simon.

I made a list of what I thought Sanda needed, but I didn't know what DSS had already purchased, and I wanted her to have as much say as possible in anything I bought for her.

When I woke up the next morning I had a text from Simon. "Monkton spent a year in US as part of university journalism training. He did an internship at a small newspaper in Virginia. He thinks there was some problem with a story, but can't remember exactly what. The paper was the Star Sentinel. Would have been summer of 1988."

I made coffee and tried to wake up before calling on Google. The Star Sentinel still existed, I found, but did not have an online presence. The town was in southern Virginia near the North Carolina line. A day trip would get me there.

SIXTEEN

KATIE AND I went to the barn to help with morning chores. I worked my project horse. He was coming along despite my on-again, off-again attention.

Jane watched me long-line the colt and voiced her approval. "Your patience is paying off. I think he'll make something yet."

"You mean he likes not working very often. Speaking of which, I'm leaving for a day trip today. But I should be home tomorrow at the latest."

"Is your Irish friend back?"

"No. I wish. But I want to check out something, and I can't do it online."

"Not a problem, Maddie. I know you will be here when I need you, during foaling season, right?"

When I called Dad and shared my latest ideas, he volunteered to keep Katie. Although I had planned to take her, a quick trip might go better without worrying about the dog in my truck. I dropped her off and took the road out to I-95. Driving gave me more time to think and wrestle with all the unknowns of my list. I tried to concentrate on what I would want to research at the Sentinel.

I made it to the newspaper office by mid-afternoon. They kept only a few years of bound back issues in their office. No one still working at the paper was around when Monkton interned. I would have to try my luck with the local library. Microfilm was still the storage method for papers over ten years old. No one had ever updated these records to the computer.

Eventually I found the article introducing the new intern complete with picture. Monkton looked so young and earnest with his dark hair and bow tie. How would I recognize a controversial article when I found it? I would have to find the retraction first. I stood and stretched, visited the restroom, and got a drink of water before returning to my desk.

When I came back, the young librarian who had helped me had been replaced by an elderly lady with lovely silver hair wound into an attractive bun. She smiled and nodded to me as I walked by. I watched her check out books for a gentleman who appeared to be of similar vintage. They chatted with the familiarity of long friendship.

I went back to my research and slogged through another month's worth of issues. I looked up at the older woman. She was puttering around her desk. She was certainly old enough to have been librarian at the time. I thought about how to ask what I wanted to know.

"Excuse me, maybe you could help with some research?"

"Of course, dear, if I can."

"Were you living here in 1988?"

"Oh yes, I've always lived here, except for when I went to Raleigh to college. I started at this library forty-two years ago. What did you want to know?"

"A friend of mine worked for the local newspaper. He was an intern that year, and something happened that is still causing repercussions. I told him I'd try to find the article. His name was Monkton, I don't know if you would remember..."

Her blue eyes sparkled. "Oh, Lordy, the South African boy.

Every girl in town knew who he was. So handsome. And that accent. But he did get in a few scrapes. Not knowing the culture, you see, and not knowing the important local families."

She paused to reminisce. "There was a scandal... let me think." She tapped her pen on a scratch pad as she looked down.

"Oh, one thing was the Shirley girl. That was so sad. She was from an old family, very well thought of in these parts. But she was sheltered, you might say. Everyone assumed she would marry the Lee boy. He was spoiled. His father died, you see, and his mother gave him everything. Then a good looking Army lieutenant came to town, spent his furloughs with his aunt who lived here. I believe he was stationed at Fort AP Hill. He met Donna Jo Shirley at a concert in the park. It was love at first sight. She dropped Austin Lee faster than a hot potato.

"Austin couldn't take it. After the Army guy left, his obituary appeared in the paper. Turned out it wasn't true. Everyone was sure Austin did it. Donna Jo didn't even try to check it out. Got her dad's loaded pistol from his study and shot herself. Turns out she was pregnant with the serviceman's child."

I gasped. "How awful for everyone. I guess her family blamed the newspaper?"

"Not only her family. Austin Lee's mother wasn't quite right. She kept saying that Austin and Donna Jo had made up, that he was crushed, and there was no way he would have sent in that false report. Claimed it was the lieutenant, got cold feet and did it to get out of marrying her. And the lieutenant didn't show up for the funeral. But you know, he might never have known about it. Seems like he was about to ship out last time he visited. The paper apologized, of course. But Monkton had already gone back to school the week the paper came out. Lordy, I'll bet he never even knew what happened."

"Does Austin still live around here? Or any of Donna Jo's family?"

"Austin inherited a fortune when his mother died, and he couldn't wait to see this town in his rearview mirror. Donna Jo's parents split up—each blaming the other. Her dad blamed her mom for letting her fall in love with the lieutenant, and her mother couldn't get over the fact that her husband left a loaded gun lying around. Her brother was devastated. He doted on Donna Jo. I don't know where he ended up, either."

The librarian narrowed down the time period and helped me find the edition with Donna Jo's obituary. Her brother's name was Dan Shirley. She couldn't remember the lieutenant's name and didn't know anyone who might. His aunt had died a few years back and maybe one of her relatives still lived in the house. "I'll tell you one thing. Whoever's living there doesn't keep it up like Miss Mamie did. She was Mamie Johnson. But the nephew was her sister's boy. Had a different name. I never knew her children—could be one of them lives there."

I tried to find the fake obituary and the retraction, but couldn't locate either.

I made sure I had written down everything so I could read it and thanked her for her help. Simon would have more resources to track down Austin Lee or Dan Shirley, but maybe I could at least get a name for the lieutenant.

The cloudy day had changed to a rainy one, with gusts of wind picking up scattered leaves. I followed the librarian's directions to the edge of town. A badly paved side street narrowed and made a right angle turn. Tall pines and hardwoods shadowed both sides. The pavement changed to gravel. I began to wish Katie were with me. The rain had increased, and the trees were swaying. I couldn't see more than a few feet in front of me. My truck bounced in a pothole and the lights hit a rusty mailbox. A sandy lane led into the woods.

I stopped, pondering my next action. Was this really a good idea? No one knew where I was. I convinced myself that the weather had me spooked. I would not likely be back this way, so I might as well see if anyone lived here. I wasn't feeling any kind of premonition, just the circumstances and common sense. There was no name on the mailbox, only a crudely printed number.

I put the truck in low gear and headed down the lane, branches and brambles scratching the side as I went. "No trespassing" and "Dead End—Private Drive" signs appeared on both sides. Acorns or something hit the roof. The lane ended in a small clearing with a log house set back in the trees. The rain had diminished to a fine mist. A porch light came on and a figure stepped out the door, holding what looked like a shotgun.

I decided to stay in the truck, but cracked the window and shut off the engine so he/she could hear me. "Sorry to bother you," I yelled. "I'm looking for a relative of the lady who used to live here."

He (I guessed) stepped off the porch. "She's been dead a long time. What do you want?"

"I'm trying to find her nephew, the one who was in the service and used to visit her."

He turned and spat to the side. "Good riddance to bad rubbish. Don't know where he ended up. He shipped out to the Middle East and came back messed up. On drugs and crazy. He never got over knowin' that girl shot herself."

"I'm so sorry. Can you tell me his name?"

"Who are you, anyway? You lookin' for him, and you don't know his name? What's this about? Wait, you don't have money for him, do you? I'm probably his closest relative. He's my half-brother." He started walking closer.

"No, no, nothing like that. I'm a writer—I thought the whole story might need to be told, set the record straight." I put my hand on the key, ready to crank the starter.

"Might better be forgotten, not stirred up. But it won't hurt either of us none." He pointed the shotgun at the ground and walked a few steps closer. "Last I heard he was homeless, living on the streets in Boston. I got a letter once, from some mission up there. His name is Jonathon Perkins. It was after our aunt died. Somehow he found out and wanted me to know he was still alive. The place reminded me of her. St Patrick's that's it—she always celebrated St. Patrick's Day in a big way. She was born in Ireland."

Odd how Ireland kept coming up. Could the lieutenant have ended up there? Didn't seem likely.

"You want to come in? Place is kinda messy, but I got some beer."

The smell of beer and unwashed body hit me as he moved still closer.

"No thanks, I've got to get back, someone's waiting for me." I started the truck then and began turning the wheel to circle back out the drive. I tensed as he raised the gun, but he took it around and aimed at something off to his right. I heard the boom as a deer ran out through the underbrush and crossed the drive in front of me.

SEVENTEEN

I WASTED NO time exiting the driveway. My sweaty palms gripped the steering wheel as I swung around the ninety degree turn onto the gravel road without stopping. By the time the gravel became potholed pavement, I had slowed and my breathing had more or less come back to normal. I had a lead on the lieutenant. And a story to tell when I could stop shaking and laugh about the crazy old coot.

The wind had eased, and the rain had settled into a light drizzle. I found the interstate and stocked up on junk food for the drive home. I wasn't the slightest bit sleepy. I called Dad to tell him I was driving home, but would probably just pick up Katie later the next day.

"You sound wired. Find out anything?"

"Yeah, I'll tell you when I see you. I need to sort out a few things mentally."

Apparently I had never been in any danger, or least he hadn't picked up on it. Good to know. I put in my Meatloaf CD and cranked up the volume.

I'd been driving for about an hour when the phone rang.

"Ms. Madelaine, this is Sanda. I hope I did not awaken you or that you are not eating your dinner or..."

"Hi, Sanda. I'm driving—you didn't wake me, and I'm glad to hear from you."

I put the phone on speaker and propped it in the cup holder.

"You said I could call you if I needed, and I have a decision to make and I wanted to talk with you. The face surgeon, he says he could remove my scar and that I would look much better. But what if he made it worse? Or what if he did make it to go away, and men would do what they did to the other girls? Maybe I should call my half-sister since she is studying to be a doctor? But I know you better."

"That's good news, Sanda. I think you need to ask the chances of anything going wrong—the percentage of risk. Did he tell you this?" What else should I say to her? She was reaching out to me and I needed to answer in the right way—to be as honest and as reassuring as I could.

"As for being too beautiful, you are already beautiful, inside and out. Your scar does not define you. You will learn, with time, how to know when people really care about you and how to protect yourself, emotionally and physically. Does that make sense?" And was that how I should be counseling her? This parenting thing was all new to me. I told her I would talk with the social worker who took her to see the plastic surgeon and get back to her as soon as I could.

I spent the rest of the drive thinking about a life where you were afraid to be attractive. I spent my teenage years agonizing over my appearance. My hair was too limp; I wasn't tall enough; I was too flat and so on. I wasn't popular, and I didn't have a date to the prom, but I did have supportive parents and close friends who filled my life. By the time I finished college I was confident about my good features—legs, intelligence, sense of humor—and I was willing to wait until I found the right man.

Sanda had been raped at least once and saw her unblemished

friends repeatedly molested and taken as sex slaves. I could understand why she might fear becoming more attractive, but how sad. Talk about putting your own struggles in perspective.

I made it home shortly after midnight and hit the bed immediately. Dad called a few minutes after I woke up to say that Joan had gone shopping, and he wanted a drive in the country. He would bring Katie out about lunchtime. I promised him lunch and decided he could help me with my cyber sleuthing afterward.

Exhibiting great willpower, I refused to turn on the computer and walked to the barn.

Jane was outside feeding grain to the broodmares in pastures. "How was your trip? Did you learn anything?"

"Several things. Not sure how it all fits together. My dad's coming out this afternoon. Do you have anything he could ride? He's a good rider, but he hasn't ridden much in the last few years."

Jane looked out in the pasture. "That bay mare, she's broke. My daughter rides her whenever she's home. And you can take your project colt. I believe he's ready for a trail ride with some company."

I helped turn horses out and spent an hour checking and cleaning the automatic waterers in the pastures. We swept and neatened, and I thought about what I would fix for Dad's lunch. I always had tuna, and I had picked up a fresh loaf of bread. By the time I walked back to the cottage, the air had warmed up nicely for November. I made a pot of coffee and had the sandwiches underway when Dad drove up.

Katie bounded in the door and ran circles around me, and Dad settled for a hug. Dipsy had come along, and she barked at Katie's antics. While we ate, I told him what I had discovered.

"Have you told Simon all of this?" he asked.

"Not yet. Thought I would email him first—easier to keep all the characters straight. And you and I can try to find the shelter in Boston and contact them. But first, a surprise. We're going on a trail ride."

"Really. Well, I did wear my boots. And I think I can still throw a leg over a horse."

We saddled up. Although I suspected he could probably still mount from the ground, I insisted that Dad use the mounting block so he didn't have to hurt his pride or his back. The bay mare was as good as promised and my colt, Rhythm, was eager but mannerly. The dogs ran alongside, sniffing everything in their path. We rode the perimeter of the farm, walking then trotting. Rhythm spooked only once, when a mare ran out of the woods to greet us at a fence. We went into the outdoor ring for a final trot and came to the middle to dismount.

"I'll be sore tomorrow, but I sure enjoyed that, Maddie."

"Me, too. We'll have to do it again."

We spent some time grooming the horses before turning them out and heading for the computer.

The mission was St. Brigid and St. Patrick's Sanctuary located in Quincy. I made a call and got a recording. After leaving a detailed message, I made note of the number and composed a lengthy email to Simon. I left out the shotgun incident.

I Googled the other names I had gathered, but came up with zilch. Dad prowled around my house, complimenting my décor. He hadn't visited since I had finished hanging pictures and blinds.

"Wait, I brought you something. Forgot and left them in the car."

He had stopped at Fresh Market for huge chocolate chip cookies. We sat at the table with a cup of coffee. After giving biscuits to the tired dogs, I told him about Sanda's phone call and her concerns.

"Parenting is amazing, but also tough. You just do the best you can and a lot of praying along the way. And when you haven't raised a child from birth, you think more about your approach. Since your brother was my stepson, I really worried about disciplining him, but we had a good relationship."

Before Dad left, I called the mission one more time. I reached a speaking human named Father O'Brian. I told him I was looking for Jonathon Perkins in relation to a sad story in Virginia.

"Perkins? We try to keep everything confidential here, but since he passed, I think it's okay to tell you he was here for several years. We hated to lose him. He kicked his drug habit and found his solace in helping the street people. We didn't have any contact information to notify anyone. If you'll give me his half-brother's address, I'll send a note."

I doubted that it would be appreciated, but you never knew. I thanked him and repeated the conversation to Dad.

"So, another dead end. But nice to know that whole tragedy had some redemption at the end."

I walked him down to the car. Dipsy jumped in and curled up, tired from her outing.

I went back to check my email, hoping to have heard from Simon. Then I remembered I had promised to call the social worker and hoped she was still at work.

EIGHTEEN

SANDA'S SOCIAL WORKER, Nancy, was young enough to still be enthusiastic, but mature enough to be efficient at her job. She knew what questions to ask and never took the answers at face value. Above all, Nancy was a good listener and great judge of character. These traits enabled her to work the system to the benefit of her charges.

She had spoken with the plastic surgeon and asked about the risk. He had assured them that the worst case scenario would be a slight improvement. He was hoping he could repair the scarred tissue to a thin line. He wanted to schedule for early January. Sanda had also had an orthopedic consult on her leg, but hadn't yet met back with that doctor.

Nancy assured me that Sanda's Medicaid card would cover the cost. I made notes to put in her medical file while I listened.

I had just hung up when Simon called. "Good work on those names, luv."

"Sanda's afraid to have surgery for fear she'll be raped," I blurted out.

"What? You mean in the hospital?"

I realized I wasn't making sense. "No, I'm sorry. Afterward, if she looks more attractive. I'll tell you later. But how are you? Did you find our master criminal?"

"Austin Lee owns Image Set, a successful international advertising agency with branches in Ireland, the UK, and South Africa, so he bears more investigating. And Dan Shirley is a Thoroughbred trainer, international caliber, so again worthy of closer scrutiny."

I was pleased that my snooping might be paying off. "Sounds like you've been busy."

"I have indeed. But not too busy to miss you, Maddie. I know you're concerned about Sanda, any word about when she will actually move in with you?"

"Should be after her next court date, maybe two weeks. Simon, I'm so worried I won't know the right thing to do or say. I told her she was already beautiful, inside and out, and that she would learn who was trustworthy."

"Maddie, you, and we, actually, will be great parents. We've seen too much of the world not to be. And I'm sorry I'm not there by your side, but it sounds as if you're handling things well. Follow your instincts."

"I'm trying. God, I miss you."

"I had hoped I might make it back for your Thanksgiving, but I can't. Do you have your ticket for Christmas yet? Will Sanda be coming with you? I could get that as part of your Christmas gift." I looked up at the calendar hanging on my kitchen wall. Thanksgiving was less than two weeks away and December was coming fast.

"Thank you, but no, I can manage. I think DSS is approving a trip for Sanda to visit her half-sister at her adoptive parents' home. As soon as I have her schedule I'll book a ticket. Changing the subject, did Monkton know about the Lee girl's suicide in Virginia after the false obituary ran?"

"No, and he's taking it hard. Said he might deserve the harassment for that mistake, but not his son and not Will. By the way, Will made it safely home, and his wife is home as well. The pregnancy is still on track with the baby due end of December."

I was glad for Will and his wife. I hoped they were now out of danger.

"What about Roger Monkton? Has the attorney turned up anything in his defense?"

"If I can tie in some of the international incidents, it would help. And you might be able to assist with that."

"How?"

"Turns out Brian's family lives in North Charleston. They're finally having a memorial service next weekend. The investigator for Roger's lawyer is coming down. I wondered if you might go with her."

"I'm not sure how it would help, but I'm certainly willing. Give me her number and I'll try to set something up."

"Interesting development from Kentucky as well. The Lexington police have recovered one of the raw diamonds. A less than genius member of the 'Lexington Mafia' took a stone to have a ring made for his intended. The jeweler had seen the alert on the missing diamonds and called it in. That doesn't really tie in to Roger's case, but it makes the whole deal more complicated."

I walked into the living room and settled in my chair, grabbing my notebook. "Did they arrest him?"

"Not yet. They're hoping for a few more diamonds to surface. But the police passed the diamond on to your geology professor friend to analyze. Turns out it isn't exactly a South African diamond."

"You mean it's not real?"

"It's real, but it has a mineral composition that's unique to a mine in Zimbabwe operated by the Chinese. I can't say any more about that angle, we're still working on it."

My head was spinning. What Simon had originally thought was an arms' smuggling operation was an information planting scheme with broad international repercussions.

NINETEEN

I MET JANET Johnson, the investigator, at a Starbucks near the airport. She was a tall, slender blonde, wearing a navy suit for the memorial service. I hadn't much in the way of dress clothes, but I had put on black slacks and boots with a sweater.

We ordered our coffee and found a table. "Thanks so much for going with me," Janet said. "No matter how often I have to do this, I hate attending funerals and interviewing relatives of murder victims. But the fact that you were there for the discovery of the body makes you someone they want to talk with."

I shuddered, remembering the grisly scene. "Nothing I could tell them would bring comfort. How much family did he have?"

Janet pulled out a small notebook. "His father left home shortly after Brian was born. His mother died of breast cancer when Brian was twelve. His grandmother, Beverly Sims, raised Brian and his older brother. The brother, James, thoroughly disapproved of Brian. Wages of sin and all that. But the grandmother called our office and said she wanted to talk to Roger. Was sure he hadn't killed Brian. Beyond that I don't know."

No wonder Brian had been needy. I felt a cloud of depression and ickiness closing around me. Wished I could leave, but I believed

Roger's story, and I needed to help in any way I could.

Janet drove her rental, using the GPS on her phone. We found the small, brick church with opaque yellow windows and no redeeming charm. A small group of mourners gathered in the parking lot and made their way into the church. We waited until a few minutes before the service was supposed to start and quietly slid into a back pew.

A few terribly off-key hymns were sung without benefit of organ or piano before the minister stepped forward. I was already cringing inside, expecting a hellfire and damnation sermon. But the preacher surprised me with a sermon on mercy, on people surviving the best they could with the lot they had been given in life. I watched an erect, dignified older woman in the front pew. She cried softly but never slumped in her seat. The man beside her squirmed and fidgeted, frequently wiping his forehead with a starched hankie as he glanced around. The woman on the far side of him sat stiffly, as if waiting for an explosion.

The preacher asked if anyone else cared to speak and the brother strode purposefully to the podium.

"Thank you for coming," James said, "to comfort our family. But in reality, we know that Brian had all but chosen his fate by living a sinful lifestyle. I hope that others will learn from his death." With that he walked proudly back to the pew, oblivious to the shock and horror of some of the mourners. Others were nodding "Amen."

The preacher said, "The women of the church have prepared refreshments in the fellowship hall, please join us."

Janet and I scooted out the back, right after the family exited through a door at the front of the church.

"I need to walk around the block and cool off before I punch that obnoxious SOB." She stopped, took a deep breath, and looked at the ground. "I'm sorry. That was unprofessional."

"Not to worry, I feel the same. But I'm sure he's sincere. And he, too, was a victim of his circumstance. He definitely creeps me out."

We waited for most of the mourners to pass through a receiving line of sorts inside the fellowship hall door. We had decided to introduce ourselves as friends of Roger's family. They might kick us out on sight, but that seemed better than saying we were investigators working to clear Roger. I looked around at the crowd and wondered if the prosecutor had anyone in attendance. The stark white walls and glaring fluorescent lights were not welcoming. The lack of windows made me feel claustrophobic.

James and his wife were engaged in a conversation when we got to his grandmother. We introduced ourselves and she brightened. "Oh, thank you for coming. I wanted to talk with you. I know Roger can't have killed him. Help yourselves to something to eat, and I'll try to get with you later."

James was so earnestly conversing that he didn't notice as we swung away from him and headed for the food. My anger and nerves were making me really hungry, and there was plenty to be had.

We found a seat in the corner of the room and hoped we wouldn't be accosted by curious congregation members. Mrs. Sims graciously made her way across the crowd, smiling and hugging, the epitome of a southern lady. At a friend's insistence she sat and ate a few bites before excusing herself and walking toward us.

"Mrs. Sims, we are so sorry. And we are grateful for anything you can tell us," Janet said as she stood to face Brian's grandmother.

"Roger brought that boy more happiness than I ever could. But I know there were troubles. Brian told me he hadn't been entirely honest with Roger, and it was causing a problem. He was afraid, but not of Roger. He was worried that something he had done would cause a problem for Roger, maybe even put him in danger. And I'm so sorry for what James said. He believes it, you know. But I read the Bible too, and Jesus was always about love. Those boys loved each other and there was never anyone else for either of them."

"Do you have any clue why Brian was afraid?"

"No. But I'm pretty sure it had to do with hacking. That was his talent and his temptation. Almost got him expelled from MIT. I know he had a contract with an advertising agency to put stories on social media, but lately he had been concerned about what he was posting and where, but he wouldn't tell me anymore."

"Did he ever mention Austin Lee from Image Set Advertising or Dan Shirley?" I asked.

Mrs. Sims shook her head sadly. "If he did, I don't remember. But y'all give me your cards, and I'll call if I think of anything. I know you're working to clear Roger, and I'm glad. I would love to see him when all of this is behind us. But don't say anything to James. He can't help what he thinks."

Janet pulled out a business card. I dug through my purse and found one of Jane's cards advertising her farm. I scribbled my number and email address on it.

Janet asked, "When was the last time you heard from Brian?"

Mrs. Sims closed her eyes to think. "He called shortly before he passed. He said, 'Roger's upset with me, and he has a right, but I'm trying to fix things, even if it costs me this job. The money's not worth it.' I asked him what he meant, but he told me he'd already said too much and would call soon. I didn't realize until now, that was probably the day he died." She brought her handkerchief up to her face before dissolving in tears. "I should have called Roger or someone."

Janet touched her gently on the arm. "You couldn't have known. We believe he was killed by a professional. There wasn't anything you could have done. I am so sorry."

I looked up to see James striding toward us, his mouth set in a tight line. The preacher saw him too and stepped in to run interference.

We turned and walked quickly to the door, slowing as we waded through the crowd of smokers outside.

TWENTY

JANET DROPPED ME off at Starbucks to retrieve my truck, and I followed her to the motel. "Want to come in and have a glass of wine before you leave?" Janet asked, pointing toward the motel lounge.

The funeral had left me depressed and disturbed, with a literal bad taste in my mouth. I needed some detox time. "Sure, just one before I drive home."

The lounge sported a few weary sales rep types, collars and ties loosened. We found a table away from the other drinkers and the television.

"I wish we could pin the murder on James, but I can't see him cutting up his brother, even in righteous indignation," Janet said as she shrugged off her jacket.

I hadn't considered that. An avenging angel? "Have the police interviewed him?"

"I would think so, as next of kin, but I haven't heard that he will be a witness for the prosecution. Don't know if they've checked his comings and goings."

"Still, Brian's murder seems more like an execution by pros."

We thought about that and agreed. Janet insisted on picking up the tab and walking me out to my truck. After promising to stay in touch, I took off for the farm.

I didn't want to think about Brian and his grieving grandmother anymore. When I stopped for diesel, I picked up a Charleston paper for distraction. Rush hour was over and my drive home was short.

After changing into sweats, I fixed a mug of tea and sat down in the living room to catch up on the news. I glanced at a small headline on the regional news page. "Arson suspected in library fire." I wondered who would burn a library and skimmed over the article. Not any library, but the Virginia library I had recently visited had caught on fire during operating hours. Only quick action by an employee had saved the building. I felt the hair stand up on the back of my neck.

I read the article again. "Long time librarian Gladys Smythe smelled smoke when she walked to the basement. She pulled the alarm and managed to extinguish the fire. Thanks to her quick action the building and most of the archived material were saved. Smythe was hospitalized for smoke inhalation."

Gladys was the elderly woman who had helped me. After an online search, I found the phone number for the regional hospital. I was cut off twice, but was eventually transferred to her room.

"Hello." She coughed, then said, "Hello, are you there?"

"Ms. Smythe, this is Madelaine Jones. I came to your library a few days ago for microfilms of the newspaper. I'm so glad you're okay."

"I've been better." She paused to take a deep breath. "But this will pass."

She wheezed as she struggled to breathe. "Don't try to talk," I said. "I just wanted to check on you."

"Hope you made copies of those articles you looked up. Fire started around the newspaper microfilm. They'd been dumped out of the cans. Asian lad. Asked for the restroom. Never saw him before. Didn't see him after." She dissolved into a long coughing fit.

"Please rest. I'll call you later."

Holy shit. Was someone following me? Or more likely, was this a precaution, wiping out the ties to Monkton? And why now? Had Simon's investigation of Austin Lee or Dan Shirley triggered this?

I turned on all the outside lights and let Katie out for her pre-bed pee. Then I checked each of my door and window locks. I found the gun Simon had given me and put it in the drawer by my bed. Irish time was two a.m., so I wouldn't call him. And a text might wake him as well. I organized my thoughts and sent him an email.

An old sitcom failed to hold my attention. I paced the cottage, looking out of the windows. The full moon, along with my outside lights, revealed only shrubs and trees. Katie picked up on my nerves and followed me but finally yawned loudly and retreated to her bed. I tried to read and must have eventually fallen asleep with the lights still burning. I woke with a nagging thought that I couldn't quite grasp.

I tried to call Simon, but got his voicemail.

Then I called Janet. I had to explain about my trip to Virginia before telling her about the fire. Simon had given her the Shirley and Lee names, but she hadn't known how I had come across them.

Janet asked a few questions and then the one my subconscious had been seeking. "Do you think Brian's grandmother, Beverly Sims, is in danger?"

"She doesn't really know anything, but someone could think that she does. I wouldn't have any pull with the North Charleston Police Department. I'll try Simon again and see if maybe his FBI contacts could encourage some police protection for her."

"What about you? If someone knew you accessed those old newspaper files, you could be in peril as well."

I didn't tell her I'd been up all night worrying about that. "I can go stay with my dad for a few days. I'll call you if I hear anything else."

Simon phoned shortly after. He was already working on the information I had gleaned from the files. I told him I was worried about Beverly Sims.

"A valid concern," he answered. "Another problem is that no one can find Austin Lee. I'll call my FBI contacts in Charleston and fill them in. They might be able to arrange for some police protection for Mrs. Sims. And for you."

***

Jane had received a truckload of shavings, and I helped her to bed stalls for the rest of the day. Shoveling bedding is a mindless task. My thoughts circled in a stream of "what ifs" with no conclusions. By the afternoon my back was aching, and I decided to spend at least one night with Dad to avail myself of their condo hot tub. I could also get Joan and Dad's take on the latest information.

I went directly to the hot tub and almost fell asleep. I finally roused myself to go take a shower, and Joan encouraged me to put on my pajamas. Dinner would be sandwiches in the den. I got out my notes, and Dad and Joan both had paper and pen to sort through the newest characters and events.

Joan asked, "Do you think Simon has eliminated the Shirley man, the horse trainer, as a suspect?"

He hadn't mentioned Dan Shirley in our last conversation, but that didn't mean he wasn't still investigating him. "I don't know, but I think the Chinese diamond connection made him think more about Lee with his advertising agency." The library fire, too, had the earmarks of a larger network than one horse trainer would be able to put together.

"We know they knew each other, and both were affected by the Shirley girl's suicide so long ago, I suppose they could be working together," Dad said.

I refilled my coffee cup. "The fake news planting would definitely have political and financial implications for governments and businesses. But fake news concerning a racehorse could affect the odds."

We hashed out ideas until I could no longer keep my eyes open. I checked my phone to find a text from the social worker. Sanda would be coming to live with me tomorrow afternoon. She would be with me for a month before leaving to visit her half-sister over Christmas break.

TWENTY-ONE

I FROZE WHEN I read the text.

Dad was watching me. "What is it, Maddie?"

"Good news. Sanda's coming tomorrow." Was I ready? Was I putting her in danger? Could I really be a good parent?

Dad watched me closely. "You seem conflicted. Nervous?"

In the clear light of day, I decided I wasn't in any danger. At least I hoped not. And I wasn't going to let fear run my life. I would take precautions, but giving Sanda a home was my priority. I looked up at him with a smile. He knew me so well. "Yes, I'm nervous. But I have a good support system."

I begged off breakfast and left for my cottage. Katie sniffed around the yard and bounded up on the porch with no concerns, so I followed. I spent the morning speed cleaning. While I dusted in Sanda's room I second guessed all my choices. Maybe she wouldn't like the pink walls and white trim, the black metal bed, or the comfy chair by the window. I told myself to stop agonizing and get busy.

Nancy and Sanda arrived early afternoon. Nancy had taken pictures during the home inspection required for foster parents, but Sanda had never been to the cottage. I went out to meet them and help carry her things.

"Sanda, welcome home," I said. Should I hug her? Her body was stiff and self-contained. I decided not to touch her yet. We hadn't been together very much, but our phone conversations had been relaxed. She seemed eager to come live with me. Now that she was here, would she want to live with her sister instead?

"Thank you. There are horses close, yes?"

I smiled. "Yes, and we will go see them later."

Sanda's limp did not keep her from quickly navigating the steps to the cottage. She stopped and looked around the porch and then opened the door. Katie gave her a tail wagging welcome, and Sanda walked from room to room without a word.

Did she hate it? Was she as nervous as I was?

"You can unpack now or later. Have you eaten?"

"Ms. Nancy took me to lunch." With that she took her one suitcase into her room. Without saying a word, she began to unpack and hang her few belongings in the closet which I had papered with a cheerful floral print.

Nancy gave me the schedule of Sanda's appointments and a list of pertinent phone numbers. Then she hugged Sanda and left.

I decided to give Sanda her privacy and retreated to survey the kitchen and make a grocery list. We could accomplish most of our errands at Target.

I waited a full thirty minutes and went into Sanda's room to find her sitting stiffly on the bed.

She was clearly uncomfortable. Did she hate the room? I remembered Simon's words and tried to follow my instincts. I took a deep breath and dove in.

"Sanda, is everything okay? I'm really glad to have you here. If you don't like the room, we can change it. I want you to be happy."

She continued to look down at her hands.

"Sanda?"

Tears streaked her cheeks. She refused to look at me. "Miss

Madelaine. It is all beautiful. But when I stayed in the group home, there were many girls who had to leave their foster homes. I'm afraid that you won't want to keep me. That I will do something to displease you. That you will want to be in Ireland with Mr. Simon."

Oh boy. "Sanda, Sanda." Now I was crying. "When Simon and I first knew about all of you girls, we knew we had to change things. We wanted to do more than get the bad guys. Neither of us has children. We wanted to find homes for all of you. But we were ready for only one daughter, and you were the one we chose."

"Because you felt sorry for me? Because no one else would want me?"

"No. Don't ever say that. Because you are brave and made the best of every circumstance. You were made to work as a governess at the age of thirteen, and you did a good job, despite being young."

"But what if Mr. Simon..."

"Simon and I are still working on being together, but you are definitely a part of us, however and wherever we make it work. Unless, you don't wish to be? I mean, if this isn't what you want—" Was it too soon to leave the ball in her court?

She finally looked up and gave me a tentative smile. "I want very much to be here, I am only afraid that it will not work. Nothing good has lasted before."

"Well, then. Let me get us some tissues, and we'll go shopping. The universal cure for everything. I know I will have to earn your trust. Go easy on me, okay?"

That remark earned a larger smile and a nod of agreement. We fixed our faces and set off for our shopping trip.

Sanda noticed everything around her and marveled in it. I told her to choose two sets of sheets and a comforter if she found one she liked, or we could search further. I started to go on to the grocery aisle, but she wanted my approval on everything. I vowed to be supportive of whatever she picked out. As it turned out, she decided on a lovely floral with touches of black that was perfect for the room and her bed.

We headed for the grocery aisle. Sanda thought spaghetti was the best meal ever, and I stocked up on chicken, rice, and the makings for salad.

Simon called as we were driving home. He insisted on talking with Sanda. She was laughing when she handed me the phone back.

"I told her to be sure to insist you eat your vegetables and go to bed early. Everything all right, luv?"

"I think so."

"The North Charleston police will do a few drive-by's of Mrs. Sims' house, and I think one of our FBI friends will come by your farm tonight. You might want to alert your landlord."

"We'll be going up to the barn when we get home so I'll tell her. Any other news?"

"Do you know Aiken, South Carolina?"

"I've never been there. All I know is that it's a very horsey place, why?"

"Dan Shirley has some race horses wintering there, but I don't know if he's with them or not."

"Do you need me to go over..."

"No. Most definitely not. Just giving you a heads up." His voice softened. "What I need you to do is book your plane ticket. Is Sanda definitely going to her sister's? She is welcome here, you know."

"I realize that. But she wants to meet her relative, and social services would have a problem with her going overseas."

"I'll call soon. Be safe, Maddie. I love you, and I can't wait to have you here."

"Me, too." I hung up smiling but feeling self-conscious in Sanda's presence.

Sanda was watching me. "Mr. Simon and you will marry soon?"

"We hope so, and when we do, you will be a part of it," I said, as

I turned into the farm lane.

We had no sooner stopped than a taxi pulled in behind me.

TWENTY-TWO

WERE THEY LOST? We were a ways from any B & B's that I knew about. Before I could wonder further, the cabbie opened the rear door and Beverly Sims stepped out, attired in a trim khaki pant suit. The cabbie started to remove her suitcase from the trunk.

"Just one minute, young man," she said, "until I see if I am welcome."

"Mrs. Sims, how did you find me?"

"You did give me your card. Mrs. Jones, I need to talk with you, and I was hoping you could give me a ride to the airport later. Rest assured I won't impose on your hospitality for very long."

"Of course," I said. "Please come in."

She paid the cab driver and picked up her suitcase. I took it from her and ushered her toward the porch stairs.

Sanda had already walked up the steps with the first bag of groceries. We followed, and I introduced her to Mrs. Sims, using only her first name. We hadn't talked about how she would like to be introduced to my friends and family, let alone strangers.

I unlocked the door and invited everyone into the living room. Sanda said, "I'll finish bringing everything in."

Beverly accepted a glass of ice water and settled herself on the couch. "I've found something, you see, and I wanted you to read it." She began digging through her purse and then pulled out several folded sheets. As she unfolded them, I saw they were printed and paper clipped together.

"I've always kept Brian's emails, and I was rereading them to—to comfort me." She wiped her teary eyes.

"Let me get you a tissue." I brought the box and sat beside her on the couch.

"I think he was sending me a message, in case something happened, but I was too dumb to realize it. Maybe I could have saved him."

"Mrs. Sims, I very much doubt that. You can't blame yourself, but maybe we can find a clue to his killer."

The first email was dated in July. It mentioned a trip the boys had made to Rehoboth Beach. "I swam in very deep water, and Roger was nervous."

"That line surprised me because I knew that Brian never wanted to do more than wade in the ocean, since he wasn't a strong swimmer," Beverly said, looking up to get my reaction.

"I see, go on."

She handed me the second email, dated in August. She had underlined the last few lines. "I wanted to go visit the Confederate general, but Roger was all about Washington and the cherry tree."

"Neither of the boys were Civil War fans, and I know they attended events at Mt. Vernon several times, so I'm at a loss as to what this means.

I knew that Robert E. Lee's boyhood home was not far from Washington's boyhood home in Virginia, but I suspected the passage was more about people than places. Austin Lee and fake news?

"I'm not sure, but I might have an idea. Do you have more?"

In the third email she showed me, Brian had written about a new exhibit at the Smithsonian and eating at a restaurant he and

Roger had discovered. But the last line was strange.

He had written, "Remember when we went out for Chinese food, and it didn't agree with Roger? Remember that if something ever happens to me. Only now I think it was Korean."

Beverly said, "The thing is, I don't think we ever did that. They were seldom here together, and I don't remember going to any Chinese place in Alexandria. But maybe it's only my forgetfulness."

She had a few more in which she had underlined certain phrases and made notes to the side.

"May I keep these?"

"Yes, I printed these copies for you. I thought you and that investigator could put your heads together and maybe get some clues from these."

Brian had come by his intelligence honestly. I heard the refrigerator door open and looked at my watch to find out it was after six. "What time do you have to be at the airport?"

"Not until nine. I told James I had an earlier flight so he would take me to the airport this afternoon, then I caught a cab out here. I'm going to stay with my sister in Tampa for a few weeks. She thought the change of scenery would do me good."

I had time to cook dinner and then take her to the airport, but Sanda wouldn't be able to see the horses tonight. I walked into the kitchen to see her pouring herself a glass of milk. I explained the situation.

"That will be okay. Do you wish me to help you cook? I know how."

"I'm sure you do. But why don't you keep me company."

Beverly agreed to have dinner with us and also offered to help. I invited her to join us in the kitchen and she accepted a glass of wine. Fortunately, I had purchased ready-made sauce, so I browned some ground beef and added it. Sanda set the table.

I explained that Sanda had grown up on the Turkmenistan-Afghanistan border and was now living with me. I trusted that

Beverly was too well bred to ask questions, especially during dinner.

"How fascinating," Beverly said. "I loved reading about the silk road and all the history in that part of the world."

We quickly cleaned up the kitchen. I left Katie on guard, and we went out to the truck. The evening rush hour had ended, and we made an uneventful trip to the airport. Beverly gave me her cell number and her email address, and I promised to get back to her when I learned something.

Sanda spent the trip home seeking different kinds of music on the radio. She asked about the horses she would meet the next day and if we could spend all day at the barn. When we got home, I turned on the TV to one of the many musical talent shows, assuming they were PG rated. But since much of Sanda's life had been R rated, I didn't know how careful I should be.

Once she was settled, I booted up my laptop to find flights to Shannon. I tried the usual discount sites and found nothing affordable. Perhaps I should have taken Simon up on his offer. Not only were the fares high, but they kept going up as I watched. I Googled Aer Lingus. When I typed in the date I wished to travel, a message came across the screen. "Due to recent economic fluctuations, we cannot quote a price at this time. Please try later." What the heck?

I switched to a news site and found out why. "Irish government officials deny an earlier report that Ireland will be the next nation to leave the EU. An unsubstantiated story had earlier indicated that breaking news on the subject would soon be released."

No wonder I couldn't pin down a fare.

TWENTY-THREE

I searched various computer news sources but couldn't find out much about the Irish and the EU. I knew Simon would be working double-time, so I didn't try to call him. I sat beside Sanda, and we critiqued the last singer of the night before tuning into the news.

Only a brief segment mentioned the Irish situation, but included a video of the Irish Prime Minister denying any interest in leaving the EU. Regardless of whether there was any truth to the story, once the genie was out of the bottle it would continue to appear. This type of cyber-crime was potentially dangerous and hard to fight. How do you disprove a lie? Markets and governments could topple as a result.

I discussed this a bit with Sanda. I wanted her to understand that the internet was not always a truthful source. I made a note to myself to check airfares in the morning and promised her an entire day at the barn.

The morning dawned cold and rainy, but I knew I couldn't disappoint her again, so we wrapped up and offered ourselves to Jane for the day. Sanda had lived on Katrina's horse farm in Turkmenistan for a year, so she was a knowledgeable groom. Jane had left several of her yearlings in the barn since it was so sloppy outside. We made a day of brushing, picking out manes and tails, and generally civilizing the youngsters.

Sanda hustled about from horse to horse, talking non-stop to them. The horses would be good therapy for her. We went home tired but satisfied. I tried to make sure she was prepared for school on Monday morning. She said she had homework and sat down to do it while I again searched airfares. Aer Lingus was back online, and I found a reasonable round trip to Shannon from DC. I was planning to drive Sanda there to connect with her half-sister for their Christmas visit.

Sanda was dressed for school when I got up and insisted that yogurt and fruit was all she usually had for breakfast. Although she had ridden the bus from her group home, I would need to drive her to her high school. We made it on time, and I considered the rest of my day as I drove home.

Thanksgiving was this Thursday, and I hadn't talked to Joan about what she wanted us to bring. I called her and she insisted that she had everything under control. "But if there's something special Sanda would like to have, you can bring that."

Before I knew it, school was about to be out, and I had to drive back. Hopefully, I could find another parent who lived out this way and we could carpool. Instant parenthood was indeed an adjustment.

***

Sanda was excited about her first American Thanksgiving, and she made a fruit and rice salad to bring. She was shy but pleasant in Dad and Joan's condo and willingly took both dogs for long walks around the neighborhood.

Simon called right before dinner to wish us all a good holiday and to tell me the investigation into the Irish news hacking was heating up with leads developing in many directions. The sound of his voice stirred up a longing for him, even though I was surrounded by family. My half-brother also called from Ireland,

and he promised to meet me in Shannon and take me to Simon's mother's home when I arrived in December.

The early weeks of December flew by, and Sanda talked about meeting her half-sister. She was eager, but also worried that her sister might think she was a bad person because of what had happened to her. I tried to assure her that her sister was well aware of the conditions in their homeland and grateful that Sanda had survived. We agreed not to exchange Christmas presents until we returned.

We dropped Katie off with Dad and headed for I-95. Sanda's sister was due into BWI Airport at five p.m., and my flight left at eleven. The travel gods were lenient, and her sister met us in baggage claim shortly after five. Sanda had a picture and they found each other quickly.

"Sanda, Ms. Jones, I am Jana Albright, Sanda's half-sister. I am so glad to see you both."

I could see a resemblance between the girls. Sanda was able to speak in her native tongue, her smile and animation showing her pleasure.

After a flurry of conversation in what I assumed was Turkmen, Jana switched to English and looked at me. "I'm so sorry, that was rude. I was so excited to see her. I was away at school when our village was shelled and our mother and her father were killed. I tried to find out what happened to her, but I never did. A missionary arranged for my adoption."

"How did you find out she was here?"

"Last summer my parents and I flew to Turkmenistan to meet my cousins and remaining family. I learned then that she had survived. That she had stayed with the Irish horse trainer, then gone to America for a new home. I didn't know until today that it was not a good situation. But she says that she is very happy with you and that you helped to rescue her."

"I am very lucky to know her and to have her in my home," I said as I gently put my arm around her shoulders.

Sanda looked down shyly. We ate dinner together. The girls would occasionally lapse into Turkmen and then apologize. Jana gave me her and her adoptive family's contact information and assured me that everyone was eager to meet her. She assured me that Sanda would be in good hands, and I believed her.

Despite driving all day, I was high on adrenalin and wondered if I would be able to sleep on the overnight flight. Fatigue eventually won, and I was waking up as we circled to land. As always, I was amazed by the impossibly green Irish countryside. My brother Bill and family had insisted I spend the day and night with them, and I could go to Simon's the next day. We enjoyed catching up, and I shared pictures and stories about my new foster daughter.

Simon called as I was getting ready for bed. "I can't believe you're here, and I didn't pick you up in Shannon. I'm sorry, luv. I will be there tomorrow when Bill brings you over to Mother's."

I had been strongly hoping that I wouldn't have to meet Simon's mother on my own, and I felt myself relax. "What time does she want us then?"

"Seven o'clock for dinner. She said to invite Bill and Megan and your niece as well." That would make things less awkward for me, but I wasn't sure if Bill would want to drive the hour and a half there and then back after dinner.

I thought he and Megan were still up. "Wait. Let me ask."

Bill begged off. "Actually, I was going to let you take my car. I can use the truck, and we have Megan's car. That way you'll have more freedom when Simon is working."

"Are you sure? That would be wonderful."

"Simon, Bill's lending me his car. I'll drive myself if you can give me directions." I wasn't ready to use Irish GPS on Irish roads. Who knew? It might speak Gaelic.

Our conversation became sweet nothings, and I finally said goodbye, full of excitement and warm feelings. Jet lag enabled me to sleep soundly, and I was rested and ready to face the new day when the late winter dawn arrived.

I waited until early afternoon to call Sanda. She sounded good, so all must be going well at that end.

After consulting my map, I decided to leave early so I could take my time and stop at any shop which struck my fancy along the way. I wanted to be close to my destination at dusk. I had agonized over what to wear and finally settled on a boot length black skirt with a red cashmere sweater. I had brought candied pecans for Simon's mother and hoped I might find some fresh flowers to take as well.

Peter Simon's mother was Lady Atterly. Both Bill and Megan knew of her because she had bought and sold some nice driving ponies.

Driving on the "wrong" side again took all of my attention and kept me from worrying about the impression I would make. I had asked Simon to text me when he was close by so that I wouldn't arrive ahead of him. All the villages were bright with old fashioned, multicolored Christmas lights and looked quite festive. The scent of burning peat filled the air.

Atterly Hall was a handsome, brown stone house set behind a wrought iron fence flanked with evergreens. Lights burned at the open gates and in front of the portico. Simon had always downplayed his family background, but I knew he had been to good schools. A black car was parked near the front door, and as I drove up he opened the storm door and he came out to meet me.

I hoped his mother wasn't watching our embrace, but I didn't really care. I was too needy of the strong hug and lingering kiss. I pulled away and attempted to straighten my hair.

"You look wonderful, Maddie. Come in out of the cold."

"Let me get some things out of the car." I grabbed the pecans and the flowers along with my purse. Simon spied my suitcase and brought it as well.

"Mother, she's here," he shouted as we walked into the foyer.

"Maddie, thank God you've made it safe to Ireland. I'm so glad to finally meet you. Come on back to the kitchen, I'm finishing up a few things. Simon, take her coat."

Simon set my suitcase by the stairs, hung up my coat, and we followed his mother to the rear of the house. She thanked me for my offerings, wiping her hands on her apron as she searched for a suitable vase.

The kitchen was a cook's dream with a huge gas stove and wonderful butcher block topped island. A small sitting area nestled in a bay window alcove. "Have a seat and let Simon fix you a drink. I hope the traffic wasn't too terrible."

I looked around the lovely room and loosened my frozen tongue. "No. It was a good drive. What a lovely room, you must enjoy cooking here."

She stopped stirring and looked fondly at Simon. "I do. When I have someone to cook for, that is."

I took a sip of my wine and began to relax. Mama Bear was charming. I offered to help, and she handed me a breadbasket to carry into the dining room.

Simon followed with a soup tureen. "She doesn't bite, you know," he said softly as he came beside me.

"She's wonderful," I said meaning it. "But I expect she would do battle for her only son."

He smiled and gave me a quick peck on the cheek as we returned to the kitchen.

After entirely too much dinner, we adjourned to the parlor for coffee. I was beginning to yawn in spite of myself, and Simon looked as tired as I felt.

"You two need to get some rest. And I will be turning in soon as well."

I didn't know what the sleeping arrangements would be, but Simon carried my bag into a large wood paneled bedroom where

I noted his shaving kit already on the dresser. He closed the door before drawing me to him.

"Ah, Maddie. We have to stop living like this. I've really missed you."

"Like a toothache?" I would never let him live that remark down.

Our reunion was everything that I had hoped for and much later I nestled against his warm body, so glad to be sharing my bed.

I woke to him speaking softly on the phone. "Yes, we'll be going there today and see what we can learn."

Did the "we" include me? I hoped so.

"Up and awake, girl. We have places to go and people to see."

"Uh, dress code?"

"Jeans and a sweater will do." Simon was wearing slacks and a blue argyle sweater which nicely set off his blue eyes.

Simon went downstairs to sort out breakfast, and I quickly dressed. Lady Atterly offered a full Irish breakfast, but I managed to convince her that some tea and brown bread would be great, as long as there was Irish butter. She passed me a bowl of clementines and bananas, and I added some citrus to my repast.

We were headed toward Dublin and a social media processing site to learn how they combatted cyber-attacks and traced a recent problem. The manager was expecting Simon and ushered us to his office. Simon introduced me as a colleague.

Frank O'Connor looked to be a man under stress. His shirt was coming untucked, and he frequently ran his hands through his thinning hair. "We strive to maintain as much integrity as possible," he said, "and to take down any suspicious posts."

"Are you having more trouble than usual?" Simon asked.

"The Irexit thing didn't come through here, thank God, but there has been some weird stuff, particularly in our international department. I'll call in our international supervisor, John Logan."

Logan downplayed the problem, saying there were some weird posts he had taken down, but many times they were translation errors more than anything else. The more questions Simon asked, the vaguer and flatter his affect grew.

"Thanks, Mr. Logan. I think that's all I need." He turned to O'Connor. "I believe my co-worker is needing the ladies'?"

I hadn't said a word, but I knew there must be a reason Simon wanted me to leave the room. O'Connor pointed out a long hallway stretching to the rear of the facility. I nodded my thanks and walked that way. Men and women in open cubicles were busy on their computers. At the end of the hall I saw Logan in his office cubicle, stuffing flash drives into his pockets and pulling on a sweatshirt. I stepped out of sight. He hurried out the back door.

I ran back to O'Connor's office. "Your Mr. Logan seems to have an urgent appointment."

"Beg your pardon?" said O'Connor.

Simon was quicker on the uptake. "Which door?" I pointed and took off running behind him.

TWENTY-FOUR

WAIT. **I SKIDDED** to a halt. We had come through a security gate when we entered the parking lot. I ran back to O'Connor. "Can you close the front gate?"

He looked puzzled. "Yes, but..."

"The man we just interviewed has taken off. We need to stop him."

O'Connor finally got it. "Of course." He grabbed his phone, punched in numbers, and began speaking. He followed me as I ran toward the front door.

Tires squealed as a small, white car came careening around the corner headed for the main gate. Simon came running behind and headed for his car. The gate was slowly sliding closed. It was three fourths of the way across the opening when Logan hit it. Air bags deployed and steam rose from the radiator.

The gatekeeper charged out of his hut.

Simon left his car and ran toward the gate. "Don't let him get away. Garda," he yelled as he flashed his badge.

More security personnel had arrived. They pulled Logan out of the car, and he collapsed to the ground. Simon called for back-up. Sirens and uniforms arrived. Logan left in an ambulance and

Simon spoke with the uniforms. They helped wrestle open the damaged gate.

Simon walked over to where I was standing with O'Connor. "I'll have to handle this at the nearest station." He handed me his keys. "Take the car. I'll catch a ride later." He started to follow the uniformed officers, but turned back to O'Connor. "Thanks for closing the gate, quick thinking, that."

O'Connor looked at me. "It was your colleague's suggestion."

"Good job, Mrs. Jones."

"All in a day's work, Commander."

I knew I would be a loose wheel at the Garda station. I was on the edge of Dublin with the rest of my day to myself.

O'Conner was conferring with the police. The local Garda told him they would send for a tow truck to remove the wrecked car.

I stood quietly watching until he turned back toward the building. He looked up, surprised to see me still there. "Do you need a ride, miss?"

"No, I have Commander Simon's car. How would I get to the rail station from here?"

The question clearly puzzled him. He stared at me for a minute then shook his head and answered. "You're wanting the main station?"

I had been once to the Irish National Museum and not had nearly enough time. I thought I could find it if I got to the railway station. The station seemed like a logical place for me to go without confusing Mr. O'Connor.

He gave me directions. I wrote them down when I got to the car and retrieved my purse. I found a road map in Simon's glove box and studied it long enough to have a general feeling for my location and my destination.

I spent several hours immersed in the museum. The ancient gold Celtic collars, found in a peat bog, amazed me. What craftsmanship. What would future generations make of some of the tacky artifacts we produced?

Tired of foot, but mentally stimulated by all that I had seen, I made my way to the car park. With only a few wrong turns I was on the road to Simon's mother. I called to let her know I was en route and that Simon would probably be late. He had already sent her a text. She was a lovely woman who obviously adored her son. She was the perfect hostess, but I wondered what she really thought of me. I pulled in the drive as daylight was fading.

Lady Atterly answered the door and told me dinner would be leftovers whenever I was ready, to take my time and rest a bit if I wanted. I joined her in the kitchen after a shower and a brief check of my email.

"Madelaine, I expect you were nervous about meeting me, but there's no need. I try not to interfere in Peter's life in any way, but he has been alone for far too long. I only hope you care for him as much as he cares for you."

I took a sip of water while I thought about my answer. "I am in love with him, and we do plan to make a life together. But we haven't worked out the details yet. Has he told you about the Turkmen girl whom I'm fostering?"

"Yes. I'm very happy about that as well. I've always thought he would make a great father. Do you have a picture of her?"

I had taken some pictures with my phone during our day at the barn. Sanda was brushing a horse with great concentration.

"Horses are great to heal what ails one," Lady Atterly said. "Do you know her background?"

"She was orphaned at twelve. Katrina, a friend of my husband's and now mine, was working on a horse farm in Turkmenistan and took in several of the girls. She tried to find them adoptive homes. Did Simon tell you what happened?"

"That they were victims of human trafficking and an American colonel was involved? Yes. He also said you were instrumental in rescuing them."

"Sanda had it better than many of the girls. Because of her scar, she was put to work as a governess, not in a brothel, but I know she was raped at least once on the ship to America. She—" I teared up thinking about it, "—is afraid to have surgery on her scar for fear that if she becomes more attractive..."

"Oh, dear. You do have your hands full. But I'm sure you will be an excellent role model for her."

I helped Simon's mother do the dishes, and we sat down to watch television. Soon I was nodding off, and we both went upstairs to bed.

I was sleeping deeply when Simon climbed under the covers beside me. "Hey, you," I said. "Long day, huh?"

"Yes, but hopefully productive. Tell you in the morning," he said as he nestled beside me.

TWENTY-FIVE

SIMON WAS DRESSING when I opened my eyes. Had we even slept? When he saw I was awake, he gently brushed the hair off of my face and eased down on the edge of the bed. "I'll be out all hours the rest of this week, so I'm afraid I'll need to stay in my flat in Dublin. Do you want to come or stay here with Mum? Or even drive back to your brother's for a few days?"

Simon had seen my private spaces. I very much wanted to see his. And even a few hours with him would be better than none. I watched him knot a blue striped tie that brought out the color of his eyes.

"Of course I'll come. And before you say it, I know I can't go with you to your office or your investigations all the time, but I'll settle for what time I can be with you. And I am able to entertain myself."

I packed quickly, and we snuck out the door so as not to wake his mother.

We decided to go in one car. Simon would drop me off at his flat on his way to the office. As we drove into Dublin, he told me about Logan's interrogation.

"As I expected, he lawyered up and refused to talk. He's in

hospital under guard. Our analysts are working with the flash drives. They contain some sophisticated coding. I should learn more today."

He parked on a tree lined residential street of handsome town houses with colorful front doors. His flat was on the second floor. His door opened into a small paneled foyer where he dropped his mail and keys on the front table. A living-dining area opened to the left. The rich oak paneling continued three fourths of the way up the living room walls, broken by large windows facing the street. A dining alcove sat under an archway and a small but modern kitchen opened off of that. We walked back to the foyer and turned into a small hall which led to his bedroom and study.

Simon carried my bag to the bedroom and set it on the bed. He enfolded me in a hug. "I'd best be off, luv. I'll let you know if I can be home for dinner, but it will be late. I think there's food in the freezer at least and a few tins in the pantry. Small store two blocks down if you need anything."

We kissed softly and he turned to go. "I like seeing you here."

And I liked being there. "Be safe Simon."

As soon as he walked out the door, I went exploring. The décor was classic and masculine, what I had expected. I wondered if he or his mother had done the decorating. Here and there was a framed cartoon or other bit of whimsy I hadn't expected. The bed was made with military precision that I knew I could never duplicate. I wondered if he had a cleaning lady.

I was getting hungry, so I opened the fridge to find eggs and cheese and set about making myself an omelet. I found dishes and tea and set myself a place in the dining alcove. The walls glowed in a warm terra cotta above the oak. Horse prints and a Dublin landscape adorned the walls.

After cleaning up, I explored the rest of the apartment, and as I walked back into the living room I heard a noise at the door. A key was turning in the lock. I tensed. Surely Simon wasn't home already. Before I could decide what to do, a young lady swept in with several hangers of dry cleaning. She saw me and stopped.

"Oh. You gave me a bit of a fright. And I expect I startled you as well. I'm the neighbor. Upstairs. I fetch Simon's dry cleaning when I get mine. Put in the odd package or what have you. Is he here?"

"Ah. No. He's gone to work. I'm Madelaine Jones."

"The American? I'd heard you would be visiting. Welcome to Dublin. I'll be off then." With that she hung the dry cleaning on the hall tree and turned around, her long blonde hair swinging behind her. I wondered what other services she might provide before I censored my jealousy.

I took a long walk around the neighborhood of well-kept town houses and stopped at the local store for yogurt, Diet Coke, and a loaf of bread. A small park lay on the far side of the store. Nannies and young mothers watched their charges play on the swings and feed the ducks. The smell of burning peat lingered in the air. Surely these fine houses all had gas fireplaces, not peat stoves.

I went back to the apartment and studied my Dublin map, trying to figure out where I was and what was nearby. As I looked at the map, I heard sirens. At first I ignored them as urban noise, but the number increased and they seemed to be converging somewhere close.

Curiosity won. I grabbed my keys and phone and set out in the direction of the sirens. I headed east on cross streets toward a busy thoroughfare where traffic was grinding to a halt. I wondered if it was a fire or a wreck.

On the main street firetrucks and police cars skewed in front of a modest stone office building. The Garda were erecting a perimeter barrier around the building. Was it a fire or maybe a bomb threat?

"Do you know this building?" I asked the woman standing beside me.

"Some office, I reckon."

"That's Monkton Communications," said a man behind me.

Was this related to Logan's arrest? Despite the police precautions, I had no premonition of danger.

Until Simon ran into the building.

TWENTY-SIX

AS SOON AS I learned it was Monkton's building I knew Simon would be involved, but seeing him there gave me an extra jolt of primal fear with no need of subconscious premonitions. I could hear all manner of speculation around me. "There's a bomb." And, "Someone's planning to jump."

This had to be related to Logan's arrest. Had he named someone in Monkton's organization, or had an employee panicked? Was Monkton himself in the building?

Garda on foot and mounted were working to move the crowd away from the building entrances. I had no feeling as to the type of threat involved. As the crowd gathered, I moved back and tried to find a better vantage point. A building halfway down the block housed a two story café. Moving against the pedestrian flow, I made my way down the block and into the café, requesting a window balcony table for a cup of tea. Garda were entering adjacent buildings, but no one was coming out so it must not be a bomb threat.

One man did come out: Simon. He quickly entered the building next door. Was he going for the roof? No, I saw movement on the fourth floor as he stepped onto a ledge and began easing his way toward Monkton's building. The ledge was only on the neighboring building, and I wondered what he could do from there. He looked up to the flag pole above him. The pole held an Irish flag, blowing in the wind. Before I could fathom his intent, he jumped and grabbed the pole. It didn't hold his weight, but as it broke he swung toward the nearest window and crashed in, feet first. The café patrons had joined me at the windows and someone screamed.

"He's got to be daft to try a bloody stunt like that," someone said behind me.

My nails dug into my palms. He had made it into the building and not crashed to the street, but what peril awaited him? As far as I could see, nothing was happening. Some of the crowd began to disperse. I sank into my chair and realized the waitress was trying to serve my tea. I thanked her and resumed my vigil at the window.

The café filled up, and the waitress had brought my bill. I took a sip of my now cold tea and ordered a refill with biscuits so I could keep my window seat. She sighed, grabbed the bill and stormed off. I noticed some commotion on the street. Uniformed Garda entered the building, followed by medics with a stretcher.

I didn't drink the second tea either. I nibbled one of the biscuits and placed a few Euros on the table before running downstairs. I wanted to see who was on that stretcher when it came out. Nothing continued to happen, and I paced the sidewalk, unable to be still. Another ambulance arrived. My God, how many people were injured? I still had no premonitions, but fear for Simon.

Garda continued to clear people away from the entrance. A limousine was directed to the door. Monkton walked out, a large bandage on his neck. A medic helped him into the car, and he assured the EMT that no trip to the hospital was necessary. I dove through the crowd to reach him, but a Garda grabbed me. "No, Miss, step back."

"I need to know about Commander Simon," I yelled.

"What about the commander? This is Garda business. You need to move out of the way." He took my arm and pulled me away from Monkton's car as he spoke.

Another patrolman cleared a path for the big car, and then a horn blasted as a small black truck charged down a side street. My conscious fear for Simon was replaced with an overwhelming feeling of dread.

The truck was taking dead aim for Monkton and we were in the way. Time slowed. Monkton's driver recognized the threat and threw the Mercedes into reverse, cutting the wheel hard to the right. The Garda let go of me and swung his club toward the windshield of the approaching truck. I dove in front of Monkton's car as it swung around and ran for the sidewalk. A large cart full of newspapers stood beside three news vending machines. The stock boy stood frozen as he watched the impending crash.

"Help me," I yelled, grabbing one handle of the cart. "Push this."

We shoved the cart toward the truck, then ran back toward the building. The truck hit the cart, sending newspapers flying into the air. The cart slammed sideways into the front corner of the limousine and the truck came to rest against the cart, piles of newspaper covering the hood.

Metal shrieked and people yelled. I expected an explosion. Monkton's driver opened his door and several Garda moved toward the truck. "Get back," I yelled. They kept coming. "Bomb!" I shouted as loud as I could.

For what seemed like a very long time, everyone froze and stared at me. Had I gone round the bend? The truck driver dove out the passenger door before the street exploded.

TWENTY-SEVEN

I WOKE UP on a stretcher, in an ambulance, I presumed, from my surroundings. As I twisted around to see where I was, I noticed two things: any movement hurt my head and I was apparently handcuffed to my stretcher. A paramedic was writing something. He released my blood pressure cuff and noted that I was awake.

"How are you feeling, miss? Can you hear me?"

"Yes, and my head hurts."

"It should. You have a nasty knot where you hit the ground. Anything else bothering you?"

I moved various parts and tried to keep my head still, which reminded me I was handcuffed. "Nothing but the handcuffs. Can you tell me why I'm cuffed?"

"I can't answer for the Garda, now can I? But I'm sure someone will be along to see to you shortly."

For a few minutes, I didn't remember where I was or what had happened. An accident, an explosion? I wanted to ask, but the paramedic had disappeared. I knew I was in Ireland. Simon was... where was Simon? I had been worried about him. Something about a building. But that was all I could summon.

A middle aged man slid into the ambulance beside me. He

introduced himself as Inspector O'Reilley. "Miss, what can you tell me about the explosion?"

"Explosion? That's what it was. I thought so, but I've only just come to and I don't remember much."

"How did you know there was a bomb in the truck?"

"Truck? Whose truck? Will's truck? No, that was months ago." I knew I was rambling, but I couldn't help myself.

"Who is Will? What is your relationship?"

"Will's a groom. In Kentucky. From South Africa. I knew his truck had a bomb..."

"Miss, that's what I'm asking you. How did you know there was a bomb in the black truck?"

In a brief moment of clarity I remembered Monkton. "Lord Monkton? Is he okay? His driver? The Garda?"

"Most of their injuries are superficial. Thanks in part to your screaming about a bomb. But we need to know how you knew that."

I didn't remember that. I did remember feeling strange, then a thought? A vision of an explosion. How could I explain when I wasn't even coherent? Simon could explain. Simon. Was he injured? Where was he?

"Commander Simon. He knows about me. Is he hurt?"

The paramedic interrupted. "Sir, we are ready to transport to hospital. Risk of skull fracture. Have to check it out. Do you have an officer to ride with her?"

O'Reilley looked around at the commotion outside the ambulance. "Right, I'll get an officer. Miss Jones, I have your phone and purse. But I'm leaving your ID and health cards with the driver. You will be in police custody until we sort this out. And I will be asking Commander Simon about you."

"So he's alive? I was afraid, I saw him on the ledge..."

O'Reilley's eyes softened as he looked at me. "Very much so."

I must have fallen back asleep. I woke to bright lights and

questions in the ER. Someone told me I was concussed, and that I would be kept for observation as well as under police custody. I didn't have my phone, so I couldn't try to call Simon. I drifted in and out and was unable to give them my address in Dublin.

Food aromas brought me around, and I realized I was hungry. The nurse raised my bed and served me lamb stew and brown bread. My left hand was still cuffed, so thank goodness I was right handed. My mind was clearer, and food and water helped me to feel more in control.

A policewoman uncuffed me and escorted me to the bathroom. I was a little dizzy, but I could walk slowly. I wet a towel and carefully wiped my face. She handed me a comb from a toiletry kit. As she helped me back into bed, a familiar voice spoke outside my door.

"She bloody well saved Lord Monkton's and your officer's lives, and you arrested her?"

"She knew about the bomb. She couldn't tell us how she knew about the bomb," O'Reilley insisted.

"Damn lucky she did, aren't we?" Simon said as he walked into the room with the inspector trailing behind him.

"Maddie, luv. I didn't know until a few minutes ago. How do you feel?" He bent and smoothed the hair off my forehead while giving me a serious look. I think he was going to kiss me, but thought better of it with O'Reilley looming behind him. He sat on the bed and took my hand. I realized he was taking my pulse. I often forgot he had trained as a physician.

He spoke softly. "How did you get to the building? Why were you there?"

"I heard all of the sirens. Walked over out of curiosity. Then I found out it was Monkton's office. I saw you go in. I saw you on the ledge and I..."

"But you didn't have a premonition about me, did you? As you can see, I'm fine."

The deep circles under his eyes and the haunted look in them told me he was not exactly fine, but alive and functioning at least.

"No. I was worried about you on a conscious level. I didn't know what the threat was, but the premonition came later. I was trying to ask about you and Monkton left, and then I felt dread and had a thought, or maybe a vision, of an explosion. I had to warn him, everyone, before it was too late."

O'Reilley listened. "Are you a seer, Miss Jones?"

Simon answered. "Madelaine's father has premonitions about fires, and they have saved his and her life more than once. Now Madelaine is having her own feelings, and she seems to have inherited the second sight. I've seen enough to believe her.

"Madelaine is also my fiancée. She helped me at the beginning of this case, the diamond smuggling with the horses sent to America. She also uncovered some possible suspects with long ago ties to Monkton and reasons for wanting revenge."

"With her second sight?"

"No. With good old-fashioned hard work. She was an investigative journalist before her husband was killed."

Simon was squeezing my hand as his anger grew. I squeezed back, hard.

He understood and took a deep breath. "Sorry, luv." He looked up at O'Rielley. "I also know that since I have a personal relationship with Ms. Jones, investigation of her has to be without my being involved at any level. But I think you'll find my superior officer is very aware of her role in my ongoing case."

The inspector backed up and spread his hands. "I'm too much an Irishman to doubt her premonitions, and I'm sure that everything you've said will be included in my report. She's free to go if the docs will release her." With that he unlocked my handcuff.

Simon went to find a nurse.

"Ms. Jones, it's been a pleasure. And thank you for the lives you undoubtedly saved today. I apologize for any inconvenience, but I have to do my job, and you can see how it looked."

"I understand."

Simon returned, grumbling that the nurse didn't know if the resident on duty could release a patient or not. He leaned over to give me the kiss he had earlier restrained and traced his finger gently under my eye. "You're going to have quite a shiner, there, Miss Jailbird."

I laughed and pulled his hand to my side. I was afraid he would lecture me about having gone to Monkton's building, and I was afraid I would whimper about seeing him in danger. But neither happened. We were growing up, it seemed.

We were both dozing when the resident made his very early morning rounds. He studied the chart and me and decided that yes, I could go home with Dr. Commander Simon. While we waited for the paperwork, Simon found a wheelchair and helped me into it. It wasn't until we were settled in bed in his flat that he commended me.

"Maddie, you acted on what you felt, rather than what you knew, and saved lives by doing it. I'm very proud of you."

"Simon, I don't know the details, but I know you were a hero yesterday and do so more often than I can ever know."

"Yes. Well, as to the details. One of Monkton's long time supervisors was spooked by Logan's arrest. He took Monkton at knife point and demanded a helicopter ride out of the country. Monkton's secretary had been concerned by the supervisor's manner when he asked to see the boss. She left the intercom on and then called police. I intercepted them on the stairway to the roof heliport. The supervisor took off, then dove off the roof on the other side of the building. He ended up in a body bag."

"So another dead end?" I thought about what I had just said and broke out in hysterical giggles. The more I tried to stop, the harder I laughed. Simon worked to keep a straight face but before long he was laughing as hard as I was.

When we could catch a breath, he said, "We have his phone. He tried to wipe his computer and laptop, but I think our tech team can salvage his contacts. We'll search his home tomorrow. Or today, rather. We'd best get a nap. No. I shouldn't let you sleep very long. An hour, then."

He woke me in an hour and a half with coffee and toast. He checked my eyes and vison as well as balance and made me swear I would not leave the bed or couch except for a shower, taken while he was still at home. I readily complied and asked if I could sleep now.

I woke again at noon and wondered how Simon was functioning on almost no sleep.

He made it home with dinner around five. He told me about his day as he set out containers of Chinese take-out. "James Kennedy was his name. He worked for Monkton for twenty years. His treason really hit Monkton hard. He'd brought Kennedy into the investigation of news planting and considered him as his right hand man in Ireland. Turned out he was right handy at covering up his part."

"Does Monkton know why he did it? For money?"

"Probably. Kennedy's wife left him to marry a rich British golfer about five years ago. Kennedy took it hard. Decided that getting rich was the best revenge. He worked lots of extra hours and Monkton was about to offer him a share in the company. But he was greedy. When someone approached him, he was ready and willing. His flat was cleaned out. No forwarding address. I expect we'll find offshore accounts and a nice hidey hole."

"Are you any closer to knowing who's at the top of this scheme?"

"A lot like an onion, we keep peeling off layers to find more rot underneath. But passport control reported that Dan Shirley just entered the country, supposedly to race at Limerick at Christmas."

"Do they have flat racing this time of year?"

"No, it's all chasers, which makes it more interesting, since there's no record of him ever having trained a steeplechase horse. Of course, he could be coming to look at other horses around the area. I should know more tomorrow. Fancy a bit of Christmas racing?"

"You bet." I giggled. "We can all bet. Bill and Megan might want to go as well. If that won't be a problem?"

"Excellent idea. It would appear more as a holiday outing on our part. Boxing Day?"

"I'll call Bill."

TWENTY-EIGHT

MEGAN AND BILL were all in favor of the outing. There were some point-to-point horses Megan knew from hunting who would be racing that day, and she was eager to see them. Simon's mother was hosting a Christmas Eve Party and dinner. Planning to show me off to the family, no doubt. We would go to Bill's for Christmas day and racing the next. I puttered around the apartment while Simon was out. Eventually I came up with a recipe to make an appetizer for Christmas Eve and found my way to a grocery store.

Simon was home late but full of news. "Not only will Dan Shirley be at Limerick, but our advertising giant, Austin Lee, has also come into the country. Monkton had also planned to be there, he owns a novice chaser, but after the attempt on his life, agreed that staying home might be the better course. He did say he would be glad to serve as a target if we thought that would help to flush out the villain or villains.

"I'm meeting with my team tomorrow morning. Then we should be able to head for Mum's by late afternoon. Oh, by the way, could you run by Brown Thomas and pick up a scarf for her?"

"I've been asking you about her gift since I've been here. You said you had it taken care of. Tomorrow is Christmas Eve," I said, hearing the rise in my voice.

"Ah—I knew she wanted a scarf to wear with her new navy suit. I looked online, but I never did anything about it. Thought you'd be the better judge of what was suitable. But with one thing and another, I forgot to ask you." He tentatively reached for my hand. "I'm sorry, luv."

Christmas Eve in a crowded department store? Why not? I forgot my irritation. I was happy to do this for him. It would be an experience. "Not to worry. At least tell me what colors she likes." I had been in her home and had some idea of her taste.

"Maybe this will help." He pulled up a collection of pictures on his phone which showed his mother smiling at the camera. She was always beautifully dressed either in tailored suits or cashmere sweaters in shades of pinks and corals. And at the end, a formal turquoise dress which flattered her skin and brought out the blue-green of her eyes. Now I knew what to find.

"Yes, sir, commander. Will do. Any other little chores?"

He smiled and gave me a hug. "Thank you, Maddie. I do love you. I will try to be home by mid-afternoon, but you know it might be later."

We spent the evening ruminating on what it meant that Shirley and Lee were meeting up in Limerick. They had both been off the radar, so to speak, and must have known that their coming into the country legally would be noted. And as for coincidences, neither of us were believers.

"I only hope this isn't a smoke screen for something else I should be noting."

Simon left early the next morning, and I packed before throwing myself into the shopping frenzy. The crowds were large, and pushing and shoving ensued. I reached for a collection of scarves and found nothing which appealed. Ahead, a display manikin wore a brilliant aqua silk scarf with wonderful fringe draped over a navy sweater. I fought my way to the display and managed to dislodge the scarf without destroying the display. I made sure it had no flaws and searched for the price tag. Good thing I had Simon's credit card.

I wondered how we would approach Shirley and Lee at the racetrack while I stood in an endless line. "Hello, do you admit to planting fake news and killing people?" They were clearly letting the authorities know they were in the country. They couldn't be so stupid as to think no one would notice.

I didn't even think to worry about whether Simon's family would approve of me.

An hour later I headed back to the apartment with the gift-wrapped scarf clutched tightly in my hands. The crowds were festive outside the stores, and I enjoyed taking in the decorations and holiday spirit.

Simon was ready by four, only an hour later than I had hoped. I spent the trip to Lady Atterly's worrying about the relatives.

The party was in full cry when we arrived. Simon's mother visibly relaxed when we walked through the door. She guided me around the living room, introducing me to all manner of friends and relatives whose names I would never remember. Simon was busy catching up with the same but always looking back to see if I was comfortable and not abandoned or badgered. Like any family group, some were delightful and others less so. But it was obvious that Simon was held in high regard.

I tried to sip my wine slowly so I wouldn't say anything I would later regret. Dinner was served, and we migrated to the dining room. Simon arrived at my side in time to escort me to a seat next to him.

Winter racing was a popular topic, and I tried to learn as much as I could about the Boxing Day Meet.

"There's a new American chaser coming over for the big race," one of his uncles said. I looked over to Simon, and he turned toward his uncle.

"Think an American chaser has a chance in Limerick?" Simon asked. "Who owns it, do you know?"

"Some advertising bloke. Suppose the odds would be pretty high. Who knows? It might be a good investment."

Simon's Aunt Maude spoke across the table. "Bloody fool. Hired an American trainer who's never raced a chaser. The arrogance of the Americans never ceases to amaze me." She realized I could hear her, and she flushed scarlet. "Er, some Americans, that is."

The conversations around us quieted, and my face grew warm. Someone giggled. Simon came to my rescue. "Maddie is often embarrassed by her countrymen, she doesn't suffer fools gladly."

"Hear, hear," said his cousin Liz, and the conversation, eating, and drinking resumed.

Simon squeezed my hand. "All right, luv?"

"Yes." And I was. I liked these people.

Midnight was approaching by the time the departing guests and those spending the night were sorted out. Lots of shouts of "Happy Christmas" filled the air.

Liz and her husband stayed, and she and I finished carrying the last of the dishes to the kitchen. A young girl had been hired to help and had the kitchen in good order. Lady Atterly paid her and thanked her.

We collapsed in the den by the Christmas tree with nightcaps.

"Well done, Mum, a wonderful party," Simon said.

His mother smiled at us. "Yes, I think it came off rather well. I hope you weren't too intimidated by our clan, Madelaine."

"Thank you for a lovely evening."

Simon put his arm around my shoulders, and I snuggled against him. "Even for an arrogant American."

Liz snorted and we all dissolved in laughter.

We would open presents in the morning, and I carefully placed my packages under the tree. Simon placed gifts there as well.

We went up to bed, and Simon dug around in his suitcase while

I undressed. When he slipped into bed beside me, he held a small package in his hand. "Maddie, I was so proud of you tonight, so happy to be showing you off. As much as I've been away from you, I've no right to claim you, but I want to, with all my heart."

He had already more or less proposed. I wore his grandmother's ring on my left hand. What was this? I sat up.

He handed me the box. Inside I found a day timer, with a velvet bow glued to a certain page. I turned to the page, my hand shaking. On December 31, red ink posed the question "Private wedding at Atterly Hall to be followed by late winter reception in Charleston?"

Doubt and worry etched his tired face. "If it's too soon, if I haven't given you enough notice, if..."

I loved this man. I knew how tenuous life could be. I knew he loved me, and we both wanted Sanda in our lives. Whatever the complications, I wasn't going to let him go. My phone rang on the nightstand. I looked.

Sanda.

TWENTY-NINE

MY FOSTER DAUGHTER—I couldn't not answer it. She might have forgotten about the time difference or there might be an emergency.

"Miss Madelaine, I called to wish you Merry Christmas and to tell you about my day. Is this a good time?"

No, damn it, but I couldn't say that. "Of course. Merry Christmas to you. Are you having a good time?"

"Yes. My sister and her family have taken me to museums and movies and fixed very good food. More family members came today, and we played games and ate more fancy food. It was very nice."

"I'm glad you are having fun. Simon says Merry Christmas also."

"Tell him the same. But Miss Madelaine, my sister wanted me to tell you that I was sick at my stomach after dinner, maybe I ate too many sweet foods?"

"How do you feel now?"

"Better. She gave me some medicine and some ginger ale. But she wants to talk to you."

"Sure, give her the phone, please." Little pangs of worry gnawed at my insides.

Sanda's sister was concerned because Sanda was also running a low grade fever. As a medical resident, she was trying to rule out any serious problem. Except for the fever, it might have been a normal reaction to all the rich food. Or it could be a virus. She assured me that no one else appeared to be sick, so she didn't think it was any problem with the food. For now, she would keep a careful eye on Sanda and take her to an emergency clinic if her symptoms worsened, although there were not likely to be many places open on Christmas Day.

I spoke with Sanda again. "Please call me if you need to, and I hope you feel better tomorrow. Have fun and Merry Christmas."

Simon had picked up the box and its contents. "Sanda's sick?"

"An upset stomach, but with a low grade fever."

"But you feel she's in confident hands?"

"Yes. But I can't help think I should be there if she's sick..."

"Stop." He took my hand. "You didn't know she would get sick. It's probably a reaction to the food or a virus. Either way, there's nothing you can do at the moment."

"Speaking of the moment." I reached for the box. "I don't want to regret this moment. I love you, and I believe I need to finish a calendar entry. Pen, please."

"Pen? How about an answer or a kiss or..."

"Relax. I want to cross out the question mark."

"In that case I have another box."

The ring was the same style as the one I wore, but crafted to fit around it. A completion.

I was speechless and frozen in place. I slid his mother's ring off my finger and slid the ring on and topped with the ring I had been wearing.

"Do you like it? If you don't..."

"Simon. How could I not like it? It's perfect. How did you do this?"

"When I had my grandmother's ring sized for you, I found a

jeweler to make this. In the hopes that I would one day have the courage to marry you and that you would be foolish enough to say 'yes'."

I pushed him down on the bed and kissed him. Our lovemaking was slow and sweet. No nightmares followed.

***

"You can't wear it yet, you know. We haven't officially tied the knot."

"Has your mother seen the ring?"

"Yes. She will be waiting with bated breath to hear your response."

I returned the ring to him. "Don't lose it."

We found his mother cooking bacon. Liz and her husband were still in their room. Lady Atterly turned to look at us. We tried to put on solemn faces but dissolved into laughter.

"So I'd best get ready for a wedding, I presume?"

I went over and hugged her.

Simon spoke. "Remember, Mother, small and private. Only the rector and ourselves, and we can ask Liz and Tom to be witnesses."

After a cup of coffee, they joined us for breakfast. Simon mixed Bloody Mary's for the gift opening. Simon's mother exclaimed over her scarf and the fancy camera Simon had placed under the tree for her. She gave me an Irish sweater in deep green. I had horseshoe cufflinks for Simon. He had gotten a gift card to Liz and Tom's favorite restaurant, and they gave me a modern Irish cookbook. We played Christmas music and shared our news.

Liz was very bright and wickedly funny. I understood why she was Simon's favorite relative. Tom was quick and his dry humor kept us entertained.

We left for my brother's house at noon. We would spend the night before driving to Limerick the next day. Boxing Day is a national holiday along with Christmas which makes a great deal of sense to me.

We decided not to share our wedding plans with them, which

was difficult for me. But if we had, we would need to invite them, and I couldn't add to Lady Atterly's workload.

I called Sanda and she insisted she was fine. Her sister was busy in the kitchen so I didn't talk with her, but I assumed all was well.

After Megan's Christmas roast and too many glasses of wine, we discussed our trip to the Limerick races.

Simon said that both Lee and Shirley would be tailed to the racetrack. Lee was staying in his Dublin apartment and Shirley was booked into a Limerick Hotel. "We don't really have evidence of any direct ties between either of them and the hacking or information planting. But our analysts are still digging into the flash drives and laptop confiscated from Logan as well as Kennedy's phone records. If we come up with anything implicating either of them, we can bring them in for questioning."

None of us knew Lee or Shirley by sight, but Simon had copies of passport photos. We decided to let Megan find Dan Shirley to ask about the chaser. The agent following him would alert Simon when he arrived at the track and keep us informed on his actions.

"Monkton now insists on coming. He'll have two body guards and will wear a police vest. He has a box seat."

THIRTY

AN IRISH RACE track is a feast for the senses. Bookmakers yell their odds and write the latest on chalk boards. Vendors hawk bananas. Well dressed women sport colorful hats. Jockey silks appear in every color combination imaginable. Tailgaters lay on elaborate buffets complete with tartan blankets, silver cups, and soup tureens. Grooms walk their charges on the grass.

The Limerick track was fairly new, Simon had told me, built in 2001 by Hugh McMahon. "This farm used to belong to the Earl of Harrington, built quite a house here. McMahon bought it in 1995 or '96. The old track was on the edge of Limerick City," Simon added.

"Dan Shirley is back with his chaser. Lee hasn't arrived yet, nor has Monkton." Simon looked up from his phone. "I can show you how Dan Shirley is dressed this morning." He shared the picture on his phone. Shirley wore a raincoat and tweed cap. He had no facial hair and the bit of hair that showed between his cap and his collar appeared gray.

He pulled up a picture of Austin Lee. Lee was portly with ginger hair and a full goatee. He hadn't left his apartment yet, so we didn't know what he was wearing. We split up and promised to alert

Simon if we saw anything unusual.

Lord Monkton arrived by helicopter. Nothing like announcing the target has arrived. The man was stubborn, determined to use everything in his power to bring things to a head before his son's trial. I wondered how Roger was doing. As far as I knew, neither the prosecution nor the defense had any startling new information, and the February trial date was rapidly approaching.

Chasers for the first race were called to the start. The noise increased. Then they were off, and the crowd roared. The lead horse fell at the first hurdle. His jockey managed to roll clear of the flying hooves behind him. They thundered on to the next jump with the riderless horse running for the lead.

"Damn idiot jockey," said a voice I recognized. Bill had bet on the lead horse which went off at ten-to-one odds. "He should have won this race."

"Gee, nothing like a little sympathy for the fallen rider," I said.

Bill answered with muttered curses.

Megan walked by, said she was on her way to find Dan Shirley. His horse didn't race until the end of the program so this should be a good time. I couldn't see Simon. As I looked around for him, a large, ginger haired man strode toward the track with a petite blonde trailing behind him. He was wearing a nylon jacket with a ball cap. The wife/girlfriend/companion tried to keep up with him but was hindered by the killer heels on her black boots. He was oblivious. I felt sure this was Austin Lee, and my opinion of him as the possible villain soared.

The second race was headed to the post and spectators jostled for positions. I followed, trying to keep sight of Lee. His cap bobbed as he hurried toward the rail. And then it disappeared. He was taller than most of the people around him. Where had he gone? Had he stooped down or fallen? I pushed my way through the crowd.

The blonde woman was screaming, "Help, call 911."

Most of the racegoers were oblivious. But a few good Samaritans were trying to push the crowd away from the fallen man. "We need a doctor," someone yelled. "Stand back, please."

The man's inert form lay where he had apparently collapsed face first on the ground. The blonde woman was now kneeling beside him.

I called Simon and shouted into the phone. "A man's collapsed here. I think it's Austin Lee. By the first hurdle." I knew Simon could muster medical and police forces faster than I.

A young woman ran up. "I'm a paramedic. What happened?" She searched for a pulse on his neck while she queried the blonde woman.

"I don't know. He was in front of me, hurrying to rail side, and he just fell."

The medic asked for help to gently turn the large man over. She listened for a breath, checked his airway and pulled his jacket out of the way to begin chest compressions. But she pulled her hands away quickly, then froze as she stared at them. They were covered in blood.

She recovered and asked for clean handkerchiefs, scarves, anything to staunch the flow.

The track ambulance was approaching on the turf course. I pushed through the crowd on the rail to show the driver where to stop. Simon charged up from the other direction, flashing his badge. The paramedics hurried over to the man and conferred with the woman who was applying chest pressure, then ran back to the ambulance for a stretcher and gauze.

When Lee's companion saw the blood, she screamed again. "Oh my God, someone stabbed him, oh my God."

The attendants slid a stretcher under him as the aiding medic continued to apply pressure. Uniformed Garda appeared and cleared a path to the waiting ambulance. Simon identified himself to the blonde woman and asked the ambulance driver where they would be going. He directed a Garda to take the woman to the hospital and stay with her.

The ambulance attendants gave the local paramedic a towel and sanitizer, and she climbed over the rail from the track as she attempted to clean her hands. Simon walked over to talk with her. The race had ended and the fans were heading back to the bookies for collecting or their next bet. Would they stop the racing? I looked around. There was a sea of people and beyond that a sea of cars. The grounds weren't secure. The stabber could be anywhere by now.

Simon searched for any witnesses, but no one had seen anything until Lee had fallen and his wife, Simon had ascertained, had yelled for help.

I mingled with the crowd, listening for any useful information. All I heard was, "A bloke collapsed over there, that's why the ambulance came."

"Must have been a heart attack."

Simon texted to ask where I was and told me that he wanted to be the first to give the news of his customer's stabbing to Dan Shirley. We would meet at the terrace coffee bar after the next race.

Simon met with several Garda on the terrace.

Megan found me and reported on her conversation with the trainer. "Says the owner told him the American chaser, Overlord, wasn't for sale at any price. But he added that the horse hadn't raced much and things were always subject to change."

Simon joined us. "Unless Shirley's a better actor than I think, he was genuinely shocked and frightened by Lee's murder."

"Murder?" I asked. "He's dead then?"

"No doubt. Stabbed by a pro. The paramedic was pretty sure he was stabbed in the heart and dead when he hit the ground, but we'll need the autopsy to tell us for sure. Shirley only knows that Lee was stabbed and taken away in an ambulance. I was afraid he might collapse himself; he grew terribly pale and sweaty."

"Could mean he knows who might have ordered the hit. Any chance he'll talk?" I asked.

"We'll bring him in for questioning after his horse races. By the way, Overlord is half American Saddlebred."

"Then he has my bet." National Hunt horses didn't need to be Thoroughbreds. Many were Thoroughbred/ Irish Draught crosses or warmbloods. I knew that Saddlebreds often made wonderful foxhunters and show jumpers, but I didn't know of any Saddlebred chasers. I was thrilled and wondered about his Saddlebred lineage.

The next race was over fences and the odds were changing continually. Megan, Bill, and I made our bets while Simon went to confer with his coworkers.

Monkton left his box and headed toward the stabling area, bodyguards scrambling behind him. Where was he going and why? Did he know about Lee? I looked for Simon but he was nowhere in sight. I tried to call, but his phone went to voice mail. I texted him and decided perhaps I should try to stop Monkton from going out into the crowd.

"Lord Monkton," I cried. "I need to talk to you."

He looked around and his minders came quickly to intercept me. I could see one of them was speaking into a Bluetooth device. "It's all right," Monkton said. "I can vouch for Ms. Jones."

"Sir, where are you going? It's not safe to leave your box seat." I didn't know how much I should tell him.

"So I've been told. But look, I caused Dan Shirley a lot of grief many years ago, and I've never apologized to the man. Didn't know, until you found out about his sister committing suicide. I was the cause of that, inadvertently, and I need to man up and face him. I really don't think he's behind what's been going on, but if he is, maybe I'll find that out. Surely I'll be safe enough talking to him in a public place." He nodded to his minders. "Especially with protection."

"I understand, sir, but there are things you don't know. Simon is..."

"Simon shouldn't have to be cleaning up the result of my juvenile stupidity. I heard Austin Lee might be here as well. I owe him an apology also."

Lord Monkton was not in the habit of taking suggestions. His recent brush with death had only made him more stubborn. And perhaps more eager to make things right. The man had a conscience.

"Lee was here. But he was attacked. Taken off in an ambulance."

"What? Here? By whom?"

"That's what Simon is trying to find out, but in the meantime, he would feel better if you stay in your seat."

"I see. Well, for the minute, I'll head back there. But please tell Simon I would very much like to speak with Dan Shirley."

"I will. Thank you for listening to me."

He walked back to the box seat area while I surveyed the crowd for anything that looked off. Bill found me and asked which horse I would be backing for the big chase.

"The half- Saddlebred, of course, could you have any doubt?"

"He'll be the prettiest horse in the race, I grant you that. Say, did you see what happened with the ambulance and all?"

I looked around to be sure no one could hear us. Several people were close. "Come over here with me." We walked back toward the parking area until we were by ourselves. I told him about Austin.

"Damn. And the horse is still racing?"

"Simon thought it best to go ahead and see what else develops. He has extra manpower with Monkton and Shirley."

"Shall we go see the great horse?" Bill asked. "Then we can get a drink and place our bets."

I was glad I had worn boots as we slogged across the damp grass and soft ground. Trainers, grooms, and amateur jockeys walked horses before mounting. I was always surprised to see how tall some of the jockeys were. Steeplechasers and hurdlers were older than flat racers and carried more weight, so a jockey didn't need to be as diminutive as in flat racing. For the most part the horses were bigger boned and heavier as well.

We commented on several horses before I spotted Simon standing beside Dan Shirley. They were watching a groom walk Overlord, who was attracting a crowd. The horse was light chestnut with a flaxen mane and tail. He appeared well mannered, but he was prancing and flagging his tail in the air, clearly excited by his surroundings.

"He'll use up all his steam showing off," someone said. "He's a bloody show horse, not a chaser."

I could understand his viewpoint. Most of the other horses were quietly walking. I looked at Overlord again. He had a fine head and neck but he was long legged and broad chested. His nostrils were flared but there wasn't a drop of sweat on him.

I'd once had a show horse who spent the hour before her performance breathing deeply and flaring her nostrils. She had a ton of heart, and I suspected Overlord did too. Researchers had pegged bloodlines which shared Secretariat's big heart gene. Whatever Overlord's bloodlines, I suspected he shared the genetics.

Simon saw us, nodded, but continued his conversation with the trainer. Shirley never took his eyes off his horse.

We walked back toward the grandstand. Megan joined us, and we went to place our bets and find a good vantage point. Although this track was fairly new, Megan told me there had been racing in Limerick since 1790. No wonder the Shannon Airport Christmas Festival attracted such a crowd. I wished the Carolinas had pari-mutuel racing.

Chasers for the big race were coming into the paddock. The noise level rose. Overlord's jockey was up. He was prancing and snorting but not sweating. I decided he'd either win it hands down or be totally outclassed. He was going off at thirty to one odds. If he did win, I'd have a nice bonus for my day at the races.

Simon was sticking beside Shirley. The horses paraded to the post, and they were off.

THIRTY-ONE

AT THE FIRST fence Overlord was running in the middle of the pack. His distinctive coloring made him easy to spot. He jumped cleanly and kept his place. By the third fence the pack was thinning out with Overlord running fourth. The favorite, a steel gray, had moved to the lead. The crowd shouted with a deafening roar. As they approached the last fence, Overlord made his move. His decent stride lengthened to extraordinary. He found a gap to the inside and bolted through it, moving to third. Then he swung to the outside and passed the second place horse. He cleared the last fence even with the gray. He shortened a stride, and I caught my breath. But he launched forward and passed the leader for the win.

"He did it!" I yelled as people either rejoiced or lamented. We pushed our way toward the winner's circle. A jockey ran onto the track and I thought nothing of it. He was also headed toward the winner's circle. I could see his silks weaving through the crowd as he dove around those in front of him. The crowd parted, they assumed he was on an important errand. Something didn't ring true. Then, it hit me. He ran onto the track wearing mud-spattered goggles. Wouldn't he have lifted them? A crowd surrounded

Shirley and Simon. Garda members, I hoped.

The jockey had disappeared. I searched for Simon and Shirley. They were entering the winner's circle when the trainer stumbled and Simon caught his arm. I tried to get closer. A groom took hold of Overlord and turned him around for the trophy presentation picture.

Shirley was definitely leaning on Simon. Was he ill? Simon said something to the official. He congratulated the trainer and announced that the owner had been taken ill and would not be there for the presentation. As soon as the picture was made, Simon helped Shirley over to sit on the edge of the ring. Another man raised Shirley's pant leg and felt along his calf. The track ambulance was headed toward the group. As the crowd parted, the jockey I had seen earlier now casually walked away from the crowd and still wore his mud spattered goggles.

Simon was busy taking care of the trainer, and I didn't know how to contact any of the Garda with him. I turned and followed the jockey. He was headed toward the changing room but detoured to place something in a trash can. Should I follow or look in the trash? I assumed I wouldn't be welcome in the changing room, so I tried to make a mental note of the color of his silks as he moved forward and I veered for the can.

The can was nearly full of food wrappers, empty cups and worthless race tickets. I stirred the mess gently and then I saw it. A syringe had fallen into a beer cup. I grabbed the cup and ran back toward the ambulance. Shirley had been strapped to a gurney and they were closing the doors. Simon and another man were running for the car park. I took off after them and yelled his name, but there was too much noise. I gasped for air and tried to ignore the stitch in my side.

The feature race was over and the exodus from the car park had begun. Cars pointed in all directions honking and diving into any opening. I saw Simon wave to a Garda car and I pummeled after him, praying that I wouldn't be run over before I got his attention. I yelled but the noise of engines and honking horns was too loud. Then I saw two boys tossing a foam football back and forth as they headed toward their vehicle. I grabbed one boy's arm.

"I'll give you a Euro if you can hit that man over there by the Ford." I fished a Euro note out of my pocket and waved it in front of him.

"That man in the tweed coat?" he asked.

"Yes. Please hurry."

He scrunched up his face, squinted and threw. The ball sailed right in front of Simon and he turned back to look. I handed the note to the boy and waived frantically at Simon. He saw me and stopped long enough for me to catch up.

I was gasping for air as I handed him the cup. "Syringe in garbage."

"What—oh. You think it was used on Dan Shirley?"

"Yes, a jockey..."

He took hold of my elbow. "Come with me."

The other Garda had stopped to wait on Simon and the three of us ran between cars until we reached the Garda vehicle. The driver turned on lights and sirens, and we wove our way out of the melee.

I was still gasping for air. He handed me a water bottle. "Take your time and tell me."

"I saw a jockey working his way toward the winners' circle. But he had mud covered goggles still pulled down over his eyes. That was strange. So I started to follow him. Then he disappeared—thinking about it, he must have scooted down because he was tall enough that I still should have been able to see him. Then Dan Shirley faltered. I thought the jockey might have stabbed him or something. When I spotted the jockey again, coming back toward the grandstand, I turned to follow him. He deposited something in the trash bin and I thought I'd see if I could find out what it was. That's when I found the syringe—don't know if that's related or not, but you'd better have it in case."

"Brilliant. Shirley said he felt a prick in his leg and then he began to collapse. Now we'll know what the jockey injected him with. Hang on."

We hit the highway turn on two wheels and sped toward Limerick City and the nearest hospital. Simon radioed my description of the jockey and his silks to the Garda agents still at the racetrack. We raced to the emergency car park and Simon jumped out, hypodermic bearing cup in hand. I got out and made my way to the waiting room. I found a snack machine and refueled with a candy bar while I waited. And waited. I called Bill to let him know where we were and to go home without us.

At eight o'clock Simon texted to ask where I was. He came out to the waiting room. "Thanks to you, I believe he'll make it. Injected with a massive dose of Xylazine. Easy enough to find in a stable. But since they knew what it was, they were able to counteract it quickly. He's not awake yet, probably be morning before I can talk to him. But he's under guard."

"Any word on finding the jockey?"

"No one knows his identity. Apparently he wasn't registered to ride in any race. Some of the other jockeys saw him. Said he was tall, with Asian features. They all wondered who he was. Do you remember if he was wearing gloves when you saw him? There were no fingerprints on the syringe."

"Sorry, but I didn't see his hands."

"He would have been a pro. No need to be sorry. I'm so glad you found the syringe. Dan Shirley owes his life to you. I'll be sure to point that out when we talk with him tomorrow. Speaking of which, we might as well try to find a hotel here so we can talk with him first thing. Or did you want to go back to your brother's tonight?"

"Not at this hour, not if we can find a room."

We spent the night near Shannon airport and returned to

Limerick City the next morning. I tried to call and text Sanda to see how she was feeling, but got no response. I hoped no news was good news.

***

Shirley was eating his breakfast when we arrived at the hospital. He looked pale and tired, but he was tucking into a full Irish breakfast.

Simon got right to the point. "Glad to see you awake. You owe your life to my friend, and I think it's clear that you need protection. Time to tell us what's really been going on."

"I—I met up with Austin Lee a few months after my sister's funeral. He blamed her suicide on the newspaper article and held the intern Monkton responsible. He sued the newspaper, but the court ruled there was no malicious intent, only an understandable lack of due diligence. Monkton was gone, and I thought it was time to move on. Then last year Austin Lee called me out of the blue. Said we could give Monkton some of his own medicine by planting fake news here and there in his media outlets."

"Did you know that Lord Monkton was the former newspaper intern?"

"I had no idea, until Austin told me. He also said that he'd acquired a sponsor who was willing to pay for us to plant certain news stories. A few weeks after that he called and said he wanted to invest in some race horses, thought he could launder money that way."

"You were aware that you could be held accountable?" Simon asked.

"At first he said that I wouldn't be doing anything illegal. He asked me to send him a bill for buying and training a good American chaser. I mean, I do all right, but this was found money, you know? I told him I only trained flat runners, but he insisted I find him a steeplechase horse."

I had been standing quietly in the background, but my curiosity got the better of me. "Where did you find this horse?"

"One of my clients in Lexington has a Saddlebred operation as well as Thoroughbred. They had an old show mare they couldn't get in foal until one night a Thoroughbred yearling got loose. Jumped two fences to get to her. Sure enough she turned up in foal. Overlord was the result. The owner's daughter had been training him and trying to hunt him, but he was too strong for her.

"Her dad was afraid she'd get hurt, and he wanted to sell the horse, cheap enough, as a crossbred. Told him I'd ask around and then I heard from Austin. Thought I'd at least look at the horse. I took a jump jockey with me. When I saw his stride and the way he jumped, I knew he was something special, but I wasn't sure we'd be able to rate him."

I wanted to ask more about the horse but Simon shot me a look and I closed my mouth.

Simon asked, "So he paid you for the horse?"

"Yes, in cash. It was a little unusual, but I take payment in any form. Then he paid the first training bill in diamonds, uncut stones. I told him to write a check next time."

"Where did he give you the diamonds?"

"In Lexington. I was racing at Keeneland during the fall meet. He told me they were stolen from Monkton. Don't know if that was true or not. He was obsessed, you know?"

My head was spinning. Were these the original diamonds Will had smuggled from South Africa? If so, why was there a second demand? Not to mention, who tried to kill Will? I needed a flow chart. But my phone rang and I stepped outside the room to answer it.

THIRTY-TWO

"**I'M SO GLAD** I caught you. This is Jana, Sanda's sister."

"Oh, Jana, yes, is Sanda sick again?"

"Yes, ma'am. She was fine on Christmas. Then, I thought maybe it was her gall bladder. Not being used to all the rich food. But she is spiking a fever and vomiting. We are at the emergency room, but they don't know anything yet. They are worried it might be her appendix."

"Oh dear. I'm so sorry. I'll see about coming home."

"She said not to call you, not to bother your vacation, but I thought you would want to know."

I walked out to the nearest waiting room and collapsed into a chair. I asked for the name of the hospital and other pertinent information, scribbling notes on the back of the racing program which was stuffed in my purse.

"Of course, I want to know, and I'll check available flights. I'll try to get there as soon as I can."

"But if she improves and they don't do surgery..."

"Then I will still have come home for her, no regrets." This said by the woman who was planning to marry in three days. But I had made a commitment to parent this girl, and she had had far too many disappointments in her life already. Simon would understand. He had to.

Simon walked out of Shirley's room just then, intent on texting. Then he looked up to find me. "Gives us some answers and some questions, doesn't it?"

I looked up with my eyes tearing. "Simon, Sanda's worse. I have to go to her. I'm so sorry, but..."

He sat down beside me. "What's wrong? More upset stomach?"

"Yes, severe pain and fever. They think it's her appendix. I'm so sorry."

"They'll probably operate before you can get there. But I understand why you need to go."

"Do you? Will your mother? I made a commitment to parent her."

He reached up and stroked my cheek. "No. We made this commitment, and I should go with you, but..."

"Of course you can't. I'll have to see how soon I can get a flight."

Simon thought for a minute. "Monkton may be going back to see his son this week. Let me check with him first."

"I don't want to impose on him again."

"He would be happy to do it if he can. I'll call him and leave a message if I can't reach him. Meanwhile, we'll go back to your brother's and get your luggage. Is everything you need there?"

"Yes." I smiled at the thought. I'd had nothing for our impromptu stay at Shannon. I'd fallen asleep naked and eventually dug out one of Simon's tee shirts when I got cold.

"I need to check in at Limerick station, and then I'll take you to Galway. You can search flights on the way, in case Monkton isn't going soon."

I didn't mention the wedding delay by name—it was too difficult. There were no available seats for the next morning so I put myself on standby and called Bill. He said he could take me to whichever airport, whenever I found a flight.

Simon pulled off the road by a small pub. "Care for a bit of lunch? I'm starving." He turned off the ignition then turned to face me. "You won't escape so easily. I still want to marry you, sooner rather than later, and this is only a temporary setback. I love you, Madelaine Jones."

He pulled me close and took his handkerchief to wipe the tears off my cheeks. "Let's eat and get you to our girl."

I checked my phone, but there was no further word from Sanda's sister. She had promised to call or text if there was any change so I assumed things were still uncertain.

I shouldn't have been able to eat, but a smoked salmon salad and brown bread went down well with a glass of Harp. Monkton called as we were leaving the pub. He couldn't leave for another two days.

Aer Lingus texted me about an available seat the next morning, leaving from Dublin.

Simon offered to take me to the Dublin airport, but I knew he needed to be working. We kissed a tearful (on my part) good-bye in Bill's yard.

By seven a.m. I was standing in the security line, still not having heard from Sanda. I made it through and collapsed in a seat at the gate. As I looked up from my phone, a tall Asian walked past and head into the men's room. He wore shorts, a sweatshirt, and a Yankees cap. There was something familiar in the way he walked. Could this be the jockey? Or was I imagining things? I watched for him to come out. When he did, he was wearing a business suit. Had I not noticed the way he moved I would have missed him.

I had twenty minutes before my flight boarded. I took off behind him down the hallway, glad that I had checked my bag. He stopped for a coffee and I dove into the line behind him. I texted Simon. The more I watched the man, the more I thought he was the jockey. I looked around. Where was a Garda when you needed one?

Finally, a text from Sanda's sister. Sanda had been operated on earlier this morning and was now doing well in recovery. I answered that I was on my way and should see them that evening. I checked the time. My boarding time was approaching, and I didn't know where the jockey was going.

I bought a bottle of water and he headed back the way we had come. I let a few people walk between us and tried to keep him in sight. He went past my gate. Five minutes until boarding—did I follow? He tossed his cup in a trash can. Should I try to get it or keep following?

A flight from London had landed at the next gate and a crowd began filing onto the concourse. Several tall fellows, maybe a rugby team, were blocking my view. As I tried to hustle through the crowd, I heard the boarding call for my flight. Diving from side to side, I made my way to the front of the group and looked for the Asian, but he was gone. A survey of the gates on each side of me did not reveal him. If I didn't hurry I would miss my flight.

I turned back and tried to remember which waste receptacle he had used. There it was, beside a gate for a flight to Belfast. I ran to the trash can, removed the lid and surveyed the contents. A newspaper lay on top. I grabbed that and used it to protect my hand from the grimy contents below. Two cups had slid to the bottom beside an empty pizza box. I leaned over and shrieked when someone took hold of my arm.

THIRTY-THREE

MY HEART WAS hammering in my chest. I stood up and found a uniformed Garda holding my arm.

"Have you lost something, Miss?"

"The coffee cup, uh, I need it." I had dropped my water bottle when he grabbed me. I heard the last call for my flight.

"May I see your boarding pass and passport?"

"I have to go. My flight's boarding. The coffee cup has someone's fingerprints. Commander Peter Simon needs it. Please see that he gets this." With that I handed him the smashed coffee cup wrapped in newspaper.

He reached for the cup with his other hand. He wasn't releasing me. "Your boarding pass?"

"It's in my purse, but I have to go." His stern expression told me I wasn't going to win the standoff. "If you'll let go of my arm, I can show it to you."

I slid my purse off my shoulder and dug in the outer compartment for my pass and passport. I kept a grip on both documents as I held them up to him. "But please, sir, my foster daughter is ill. I have to get on this plane."

Either the anxiety in my voice had convinced him or he thought he might have trouble holding me for trash can larceny. "Go on with you then."

I ran for the gate and received a very dirty look from the gate attendant, but she nodded when she saw my boarding pass. "Good thing for you we have no one on stand-by or your seat would be gone."

I slowly made my way to the middle seat in the last row. There were no new messages on my phone. I put it to sleep and tried to do the same for myself.

I was flying to BWI via Boston. I didn't wake up until we were approaching Logan. The custom gods were kind to me, and I made my connecting flight with time to spare. I called Jana's phone and left a message that I was in the US and on my way.

I had planned on renting a car but much to my surprise, Jana's adopted mother met me at the luggage conveyor.

"Ms. Jones, I am Jeannine Hall, Jana's mother. I thought it would be better if I met you and brought you to the hospital. Sanda is doing well, but I know she will be glad to see you."

"Thank you so much. You didn't need to do this. I'm so sorry Sanda was sick. I know it interrupted your holiday."

"Please. I'm a mother. One does what one must—we were only too glad to help."

I checked my messages on the way to the hospital. Simon had replied. "Dumpster diving is a punishable offense. Can you not stay out of trouble? Cup gone for analysis. Thanks."

I snorted. So the Garda had actually taken me seriously or at least had the presence of mind to contact Simon.

Sanda was pale with deep circles under her eyes. Her sister was brushing her hair and helping her to apply lipstick when I walked into her room.

"You really came. I didn't want them to mess up your trip, but I am glad you are here."

"You were hurting. I had to come." I leaned over to give her a gentle hug. I knew I had made the correct choice, whatever happened.

"They say I can go home the day after tomorrow. Can we go back to your house then?"

"If the doctor says you can travel, we will."

I told Jenna and her mother to leave for some much needed rest, and I spent the night with Sanda. I waited until her doctor made his rounds. He assured me that she should be able to travel the next day, barring any complications.

My truck was still in long term airport parking so I left Sanda to retrieve it. I walked around the truck and looked underneath it, feeling silly. How would I know if it had been tampered with unless I had a premonition? All seemed in order so I unlocked the door and got in. I preheated the engine twice and the diesel roared to life.

No one took any interest as I paid my fee and turned onto the highway. I stopped at a grocery to buy Sanda some flowers and a magazine. As I headed toward the hospital I noticed a black van behind me. I made a few extra turns and it disappeared. I made one more stop, to buy myself a hamburger, and drove to the hospital.

Jenna had brought Sanda's clothes and Christmas presents to the hospital, and Sanda was looking forward to our returning home.

The next morning I took everything out to the truck and filled Sanda's prescriptions at the hospital pharmacy. I sat and waited for the paperwork for her release. She was free to go with the caveat that we would stop often and go to a motel if she became too uncomfortable.

I pulled up to the loading area to meet her wheelchair. Jenna had come to see us off.

"Please come see us, anytime," I told her. "Thank you so much, and we will stay in touch."

Jenna hugged both of us. "I'll be busy in school, but I would love to visit."

I pulled out and headed for I-95. It wasn't until we were on 495 circling Washington that I noticed the black van.

THIRTY-FOUR

I COULDN'T TELL if it was the same van I had seen the day before, but I glanced in the rearview mirror and it was behind me. I slowed up and it did as well. When I accelerated and changed lanes it dropped back but remained within sight in the lane I had just left. We were almost ready to cross the Potomac.

Sanda had been dozing, but the change in speed woke her. "Is something wrong?"

"Don't know." I thought about where I was. "Sanda, get my phone out of my purse. Look up Janet and punch call. I'll talk to her."

The investigator answered. "No time for small talk. I'm close to you with a tail I picked up about twenty miles back."

She gave me directions on where to exit and said she would meet me with reinforcements. Was I overreacting? I glanced back at my mirror. The van was pulling out to pass. I had panicked over nothing. The truck lurched as he hit the back side of the truck bed. Sanda screamed. I straightened the wheel and accelerated.

I moved to the left and pulled out in front of the van. Sanda spotted the van two cars behind me. I was now going ninety. Where was a trooper when you needed one?

"Sanda, hold on."

The exit was fast approaching. I let up on the accelerator and watched for an opening on my right. I passed a semi and saw a hole. I moved right and hit the brakes. I let off as I began to fishtail. I dove onto the ramp just as the semi honked and roared past. I braked again and downshifted, my engine screaming, tires squealing, but I was under control and the van was no longer behind us.

I made a right and another right and saw Janet's car and a police cruiser in the shopping center. "Sanda, are you okay?"

She had grown paler, but flashed me a smile. "That was stunt driving?"

I eased to a stop and shifted into neutral before plying my cramped hands off the wheel. Janet got out and walked over. "I heard you coming. Glad you made it. This must be your foster daughter. Hi, I'm Janet."

A plainclothes detective exited the passenger side of the cruiser and walked up. "You want to tell me what happened?"

I described the car best I could. It had not had front plates, I was sure, and the windows were tinted. I wasn't sure of the make but guessed Honda or Nissan.

"Let's go to the coffee shop and sit down. You look like you could use a cup of coffee."

"Sure. Let me help Sanda get out. She's just had surgery."

I was feeling as shaky as Sanda, but I tried to put on a brave front. She eased down from the truck, and we walked slowly toward the restaurant with Janet and the detective following. I took Sanda to the restroom and got her settled in a booth before ordering tea and toast for her. Janet motioned for me to go with the detective and slid in across from Sanda.

The detective was skeptical but he was working on Brian's murder and knew about the attempt on Roger. I told him I had just come from Ireland and what had transpired there.

"I never thought about them going after me or finding me, but hacking is their specialty."

"Yeah. And I suspect there's a tracking device on your truck. We'll go by the station and have it swept before you leave. Where are you headed?"

"We were on our way home to Charleston, but now I'm second guessing that. I live out in the country."

"Is there someone you could stay with, in a more populated area?"

"My dad—he would be glad to help. May I ask how the investigation is going?"

"You know we can't talk about at ongoing case, but we have Roger in solitary confinement for his own protection. I can tell you that."

I gave more details on what had happened in Ireland, and I couldn't tell if it was news to him or not. He asked a few questions and made notes. He asked if I thought it could have been the Asian jockey in the black van, but since I hadn't been able to see a face, I had no idea.

I followed him to the tech lot behind the station where the electronics officer removed a fairly sophisticated tracking device. Janet had taken Sanda to her office, and I would meet them there.

I filled Janet in on everything I knew. Simon had sent her a brief email about Lee's murder and Shirley's attack. She thought the DA's office would eventually drop the charges against Roger but felt like they needed to keep him in jail for the present.

I called Dad, and he was happy for us to stay with them for a few days. I texted Simon. Janet offered a night at her apartment, but Sanda insisted she was ready to continue our trip.

Sanda quickly fell asleep and left me alone with my thoughts. I was more than willing to share danger with Simon, but what about Sanda? She had been wounded and orphaned at twelve, then essentially kidnapped into human trafficking in Turkmenistan and brought to the United States to work as a preteen nanny outside of Charleston. Had we rescued her from that, only to put her at continued risk? My rose-colored vision hadn't included this concern. I think I understood Simon's viewpoint better now. And, I realized, I was beginning to think like a parent. I would have to discuss this with Sanda, and I could not turn my back on her, even if it meant not being with Simon as soon or as much as I had hoped.

THIRTY-FIVE

DAD AND JOAN welcomed us and offered food. I was wiped out, and I knew Sanda was, too. We consented to a sandwich and fell into bed. I was sleeping soundly when Simon called the next morning. I told him about being followed and having a bug on the truck. He was glad that we were staying with Dad but upset that he hadn't thought we would be followed or attacked. I decided not to share my concern about putting Sanda in danger and our future.

"Dad's calling us to breakfast, I need to go. Be safe, Simon."

Sanda agreed to stay on the couch in front of the TV while I drove out to the farm to work. I was distracted and edgy, nearly running a red light and having to change lanes at the last minute. I helped with stall cleaning and long-lined my project colt. Although he had been turned out, it was far too long since he'd been worked. He bucked and snorted, requiring all of my attention. The focus helped. I felt calmer and more in control of my emotions. I gathered up my laptop and Christmas presents which I hadn't yet exchanged with Dad, Joan, and Sanda.

A pickup truck was pulling into my driveway when I started to walk out to the car. I shut the door, grabbed the phone, and went to the window. No one got out for a few minutes. Katie barked, but then whined and wagged her tail. I punched 911 but not the call button.

The driver was facing away from me as he got out. He stopped and looked around, stretched and slowly walked toward the porch steps. I recognized Joe and let Katie out to greet him. I followed her down the stairs.

"Nice place, Maddy. Good to see you."

"And you. What brings you back to Charleston?"

"My lady love just shipped out. I was here for her furlough."

I knew Joe's girlfriend was a Coast Guard officer stationed out of Charleston. I also knew Simon had no doubt asked him to keep an eye on me. "I guess you know we're staying with my dad for a few days. Sanda's there, I came to work and pick up a few things."

"I've already had the pleasure. Joan fed me a great lunch, and I guess I'll be hanging around for a bit." I was relieved but also concerned. Simon couldn't always send someone to protect us. Joe might be needed more elsewhere.

"I'm ready to head that way, should we both drive?"

"Why don't you ride with me? Leave your truck here, and I'll check it out before you drive it again."

That made sense. I invited Joe in while I gathered my stuff and gave him an armload to carry.

Janet called while we were driving to Dad's. The prosecutor was going ahead with Roger Monkton's trial, and Simon and I were being called as witnesses for the defense.

"I thought the case against him was in doubt."

"It is," she said, "but Roger wants the trial to clear his name, and the DA's office wants to see what or who might be smoked out."

I told Joe the latest. He knew about our aborted wedding plans.

"Will you and Simon get married while he's here?"

"I don't know, Joe. Now that Sanda's in the picture, this chase made me think. I committed to be a parent, and I never thought about the danger to her."

"Whoa. Does Simon know this?"

"No. It wasn't until we were followed and attacked that I thought about it."

"But Sanda grew up in a war zone. She's lived through a lot, and I don't think she'd want you or Simon to stop fighting for what's right. You rescued her together."

"But Joe, she deserves to have a normal life. As safe as we can make it."

"Maddy, she is not a small child. She has lived through hell, and now she has the chance to be with two people who care about her deeply. I'm pretty sure she would not want you sacrificing your time with Simon to keep her safe. At the very least, you need to ask her."

"But I know what she'd say..."

"Then you know what to do, unless you're getting cold feet. I think it's a little late in the game for that, but better now than later." His hands tensed on the wheel and he made a point to look straight ahead.

Neither of us spoke for the remainder of the drive.

If Sanda picked up on my misery, she didn't let on. Joe absented himself to do some errands, and we gathered around Joan's Christmas tree to exchange our belated gifts. Dad had purchased riding boots for me and Sanda and both of us were pleased. Sanda exclaimed happily over the clothes I bought for her, and Joan said she loved the silver and Connemara marble earrings I found at the Irish museum.

We watched a silly Christmas movie and filled up on popcorn.

I helped Sanda change her dressing and sat on the edge of the bed as she slid under the covers.

"I'm so sorry that we were threatened. I would never want to put you in danger. I should have realized someone might follow us. I'll try to do better."

"Why?"

"Why? Because I'm responsible for you. I care for you. You have already been through so much. I want to protect you."

"But you don't understand." Sanda struggled to sit up.

"What don't I understand?"

"My family, my friends, many other girls were hurt and even killed by the Taliban and other extremists. I can't just go hide somewhere and have a happy life. I want to be with you and Mr. Simon because you are trying to stop these people. If I study well, I can help also when I am older—no one else will let me do that. I have been through a lot of things, but I'm no longer afraid to die, not if it would help the future. And if you are giving up, I don't know if I can stay with you." With that she threw back the covers and went into the bathroom, slamming the door behind her.

Words failed me. All I could do was cry. Here I was trying to be the best parent I could and it netted me a sulky teenager locked in the bathroom. Two for two so far—who else could I anger tonight?

I walked downstairs and went directly to the kitchen in search of a drink. Dad raised his eyebrows but said nothing. I grabbed a magazine and pretended to read. After twenty minutes of uncomfortable silence, he said, "Help me walk the dogs, Maddie?"

The dogs jumped up at the word walk, and I grabbed a jacket and leash. We made it to the street in silence. I turned right and tugged on Katie's lead when she hesitated.

"Whatever the trouble is, don't take it out on your dog. Or your family." The last was delivered in a critical tone.

I stopped. "You don't know anything about it."

"About raising teenagers, one of whom was a stepson? About protecting my family from the consequences of my job, about daring to love in spite of everything? What don't I know about?"

He was right. I sank to the bench on the edge of the sidewalk. "Simon and I were getting married, but I came home for Sanda. We were followed, someone tried to run us off the road. I can't put her in danger, and I can't be with Simon and not put her at risk."

"Have you talked to her about this?"

"I tried. She said if I was going to quit fighting, she didn't want to be with me. She locked herself in the bathroom."

His tense face softened, and he turned away. Was he going to cry? I heard a chuckle and then a hearty guffaw. Damn it, he was laughing at me. I started to walk off. But his laughter was contagious, and soon we were both laughing hysterically.

"Do you remember doing that?"

"I never..."

"When we told you that you couldn't go on the senior trip to New York?"

"Oh." The memory was slowly surfacing—I had pitched a snit fit.

"So, Simon, Sanda, Joe, and anyone else who cares about you and/or Simon want you to be together—all of you. Teenagers will throw fits, and you can't give in, but this is not a trivial temper tantrum. It has to do with who she is and who you are. You could all be dead tomorrow, but unless you really don't love him, you will always regret stepping away. And I believe your future daughter means what she is saying."

"But how can I keep her safe?"

"You can't. It takes a village. But Simon knows that as well, and together you will give love and life a chance and continue to fight for making the world a better place one day at a time. That's all any of us can do."

I stood up and hugged him. "Thanks. I needed that. Especially the laughter."

Joan and Sanda were in their rooms when we returned. I had a text from Janet saying she needed me in two days' time for depositions.

Game on.

THIRTY-SIX

THE NEXT MORNING Sanda walked stiffly down to breakfast and made polite conversation with Joan and Dad while ignoring me. Dad smiled when he looked away from her.

"Sanda," I said. "Tomorrow I have to go back to Alexandria to get ready to testify. Simon will meet me there. Joe will drive me and you need to stay with Dad and Joan so you won't miss any school."

"But, I want to..."

"If you are going to fight the forces of evil, you need a good education. And if Simon and I are going to work together we need your cooperation to stay where we need you to be."

Her eyes grew wide and a smile replaced the sulky pout. "I knew you wouldn't give up. I will do as you say. And I am sorry I was angry last night."

"Everyone was angry last night. Today is a better day. I'd better get some clothes from the cottage."

I hadn't seen Joe since our angry words, but we had texted and he was to take me out to the cottage. We said little, but I finally said, "Everyone agrees with you, especially Sanda. But I still have things to think through."

"Fair enough."

I dug out some court clothes and my only pair of decent boots. Joe would be back in an hour to pick me up.

I didn't recognize the car that pulled up to my door. A white late model BMW SUV parked and a svelte, bald, black gentleman in an expensive suit stepped out. He had a goatee and horned rimmed glasses. Had I not observed Joe's chameleon episodes before, I would have been frightened.

I brought out my bag and locked the door. "Uber?" I asked.

"Miss Jones, I presume?" he said without a trace of his normal island accent.

"You really should go onstage. Your talent is wasted on Simon."

He chuckled and grabbed my bag. "Have you talked to him?"

"No, but we've texted and he'll see me tomorrow. And before you ask, Sanda and I have talked as well. She doesn't want me if I'm not fighting injustice with Simon."

He snickered. "She said that?"

"More or less. Before locking herself in the bathroom."

He laughed out loud. "So she is a teenager, after all. But seriously, I gather you haven't discussed your concerns with Simon?"

"No. I didn't want to distract him from the case. And since everyone, including my dad, has given me hell for even thinking of stepping back, I have to reconsider again. What's with the car?"

"Protective coloring, my lady. I rent to suit the occasion, which goes for the suit as well," he said as he scanned traffic in all directions.

I sat back and closed my eyes for a moment and the next thing I knew we were stopping for gas near the Virginia line. I unfolded myself from the comfy leather seat and headed off in search of a restroom.

"Want me to drive?"

"Sure. I can catch up on some messages, but let's switch back when we get to Fredericksburg."

The car was as smooth to drive as I expected, and I had trouble keeping my speed within a respectable range of the speed limit. When Joe had put his phone down I asked, "What's the schedule?"

"I'm taking you to Janet's house tonight. Your deposition is tomorrow morning. I pick Simon up at Dulles early afternoon."

We exited the freeway and turned into Landmark, a pleasant conclave of brick townhouses in a well-established neighborhood. Joe had texted Janet from Fredericksburg, and she walked out when we pulled in the drive.

"Hi guys, come on in."

I introduced Joe and grabbed my bag. They shook hands and we walked into the foyer. Her house was done in blues and grays. Bright watercolors set off light wood floors and neutral furnishings.

"No offense, Ma'am. But do you mind if I check your security?" Joe asked.

"None taken. You no doubt noted the camera outside, and there are two in the rear, as well as motion detectors. All doors and windows are alarmed, and all ground floor windows have decorative wrought iron. With my job, I take my fortress seriously."

Janet showed me to my room and told me to come down when I was ready and we'd have a glass of wine. Joe whistled as he walked through the house. He was ready to leave by the time I made it downstairs.

"Simon and I will meet you at the office tomorrow. Sleep well."

Janet explained how the depositions would go and told me not to be nervous, just to answer truthfully, that I had nothing to hide. She served an excellent stew from the crockpot and after dinner excused herself to work in her home office. I went upstairs to sort through my muddled thoughts.

Was I having second thoughts and trying to blame it on Sanda's welfare? Was Sanda serious in her threat to leave? Did she truly understand the danger? I prayed for wisdom and fell into a fitful sleep. Flames surrounded me, but Sanda and Simon were outside the ring of fire. I didn't know where to go or how to get through the flames. "Keep going," yelled a voice behind me. I was paralyzed with fear and uncertainty. "You have to go forward," he whispered.

But which way was forward? And why was the voice so familiar? I turned to try to see who was talking and felt an arm drop around my shoulders and a stubbled cheek rub against my face although I could see no one. "Go, Maddie, live."

Jim! I spun around but now I could see only flames. Then a strong arm pushed me into the fire. I woke myself up with my scream. Janet opened the door, a weapon in her hand. She scanned the room before switching on the light.

"I'm okay. A nightmare." I couldn't help but sniff for smoke. My covers were thrown asunder and I was trembling. I tried to take a deep breath but couldn't draw in any air.

Janet grabbed the blanket from the floor and wrapped it around me. "Let's go brew some tea downstairs. You can tell me or not."

THIRTY-SEVEN

I COULDN'T TALK about the dream. But I did tell her about finding Jim's body in Turkmenistan, about Simon's role in helping me find the truth, and then about my fears for Sanda.

Janet listened, asking a question only when I stopped talking. "Let's go back to bed. The morning will be here soon."

I kept the light on and tried to read, afraid of where more slumber would take me. I was up and dressed when Janet came downstairs.

She looked at me and shook her head. "I hope I don't look as worn out as you do. I gather you didn't go back to sleep?"

"Afraid not."

Janet poured us each a cup of coffee and offered me cereal or toast. I declined. We set off for the office. After a morning of questions, I was exhausted. I shunned coffee for diet Coke and a doughnut. At one, Janet ordered lunch for everyone, and I realized I was hungry. The food helped. When my deposition was finished I browsed through magazines, waiting for Simon and Joe.

I heard Simon's voice in the outer office. I walked out to find him talking with Janet. "Excuse me, Janet," he said as he walked toward me and enveloped me in a hug. Then he stepped back and looked at me. "Hard night?" he asked softly.

I nodded and stepped away.

Janet led the way to the conference room and left to bring Simon a coffee.

"Maddie, luv, are you all right? Is Sanda recovering on schedule? I have news but it will keep. I know they need to finish the depositions."

"Sanda's fine. We'll talk later." I walked out and hurried to the restroom to blow my nose and wipe away the tears that kept threatening to leak out.

At seven, Simon had finished, and he invited Janet to join us for dinner. She begged off and said she would see us later. We walked to the restaurant she had suggested. Simon requested a table in a dark corner, and I'm sure the hostess thought we were having a secret tryst.

"What's the latest?" I asked.

"Before we go there, why haven't you answered my calls and only sent text messages?"

"I didn't want to distract you from the case, I knew you were busy..."

"Bull. You've been avoiding me, and I want to know why. Is Sanda still ill? Or is she upset about me being part of your life? We were planning to be man and wife by now, and I thought that's what you wanted as well. Was I wrong?"

His anger was justified, but what I couldn't take was the hurt that I knew lay behind it.

"Simon, when Sanda and I were run off the road, I realized that we were continuing to put her in danger. I began to think it wasn't right to do that, no matter how much I love you. I thought I would still be with you, between cases, but Sanda had to come first."

"Bloody hell. Isn't it a little late for these sentiments? I see where you're coming from but without us—together, us—Sanda would still be a slave governess who might need to do favors for visiting gentlemen. Would that have been better?"

"Of course not. And she said much the same thing."

"She did?"

"Yes, and locked herself in the bathroom in a sulk."

The tight creases in Simon's forehead began to relax and a hint of a smile played at one side of his mouth.

"And furthermore, my dad and Joe have weighed in as well to give me hell, and then, as if that wasn't enough, Jim appeared, or didn't rather, it was his voice, and pushed me through the flames."

"Maddie, what are you talking about?"

The waiter approached, took one look at our faces and backed away. Simon turned toward him. "A scotch, please, on the rocks, and a Jim Beam for the lady."

I tried to compose myself. "I was having doubts because of Sanda, but she doesn't want to be protected, doesn't want me without you, fighting for justice side by side. I didn't want to share all of this with you while I was trying to work through it. Then last night I had the mother of all nightmares with Jim's ghost pushing me through a ring of fire toward you and Sanda."

My drink came just in time. I took a gulp and coughed.

Simon watched me while he took a sip of his scotch. "Are you sure this isn't about Jim? About feeling disloyal by loving me, by having a life?"

"I don't think so, but I don't know. I thought I was past that. I thought I was trying to be a good mother."

"And you are. And we will parent together, with honesty."

"I'm sorry. I wasn't doubting you or that I love you."

"I know this. Drink up, we need to order dinner."

We called Sanda after dinner, and she was happy we were together, preparing for the trial.

We hung around Janet's office helping with final details. We were to be called on the first day of the trial.

THIRTY-EIGHT

SECURITY WAS HEAVY around the courthouse. We made it to the second floor, and I excused myself to use the restroom.

A maintenance worker with a mop was setting up a cone in the restroom door. She looked at me and motioned me in. "You go ahead, miss, then I mop."

Relieved, I rushed inside. I heard her close the door and say, "No more, getting ready to clean."

I was closing the stall door when the lights went out and the door crashed against me, hitting me in the face and knocking me against the toilet. I screamed as I sat down hard. She or he or whomever kept coming, shoving my upper body back against the wall. I scrabbled with my hands trying to push the intruder away, hoping to scratch or otherwise deter my attacker. As my head hit the wall, I kicked out and connected with a leg. I kicked again, upward, but the mop handle or something wooden was pressing against my neck. My purse slid off of my right shoulder. I grabbed it and swung as hard as I could. My assailant grunted and the pressure on my neck eased. I swung again. I was able to grab the mop handle with my left hand and push one end up above my head as she lunged. This time the lower end hit me on the side of the face as the top of the handle hit the wall. I threw my body to the left and out the door, but my legs hit hers and I fell hard to the tile floor. Before I could try to get up something slammed into my head.

I opened my eyes to darkness and noise. Someone was knocking. On a door? I was wet and lying on something cold and hard. Where was I and what had happened?

THIRTY-NINE

I REACHED BEHIND me and touched an overturned bucket. That would explain the wet. But I still had no clue as to where I was or how I came to be there. My head pounded. The complete darkness confused me. I tried to raise my head but the pounding increased to a jackhammer. I moved my arms and legs and decided I could crawl if I knew where to go.

The knocks grew louder. "Hello, can we come in? Are you finished cleaning?"

The door opened and a sliver of light shone in.

"Help," I tried to yell, but only a whisper came out.

I saw two sets of spike heels with rather chunky legs topped by short skirts.

"Oh my God, what happened?" asked the first woman. She turned to her friend. "She's passed out or something. Get help." She stepped closer to try to come to me but her heels and the soapy water brought her down on top of me, screaming all the way.

My chin bounced on the floor and I moaned. I could hear an increasing commotion outside the door. A female deputy came to the door and radioed for an EMT. I wanted to tell her I was okay but I couldn't get the words out or the struggling woman off me.

The deputy asked the woman if she could get up and suggested she ditch her heels.

With help, she managed to come to a sitting position beside me. I started to try to get up, but the deputy told me to lie still. "Do you know what happened?" she asked me.

I tried to talk but could only manage a hoarse whisper. "I was attacked. The lights went out and someone shoved into my stall. I hit my head when I fell over her. And I think she clobbered me with something but I'm not sure."

"This woman attacked you?"

I tried to shake my head. Big mistake. "No. She came in later. Turned on the light and saw me. Fell on me."

More deputies arrived. They helped the woman up and brought a chair into the hall for her. The deputy insisted I wait for a stretcher.

Simon arrived as they carried me out. He was looking at the procession and suddenly realized I was the victim. "Maddy, what on earth?" He shoved in beside me.

I was able to rasp, "Someone attacked me in the ladies' room. I hit her with my purse. I think I was knocked out, but I'll be fine. Help me up."

"They'd best check you out. I'll come down with you as soon as I alert the courtroom as to what happened."

"Be careful."

After lots of confusing questions the EMTs ascertained I might have a head injury, a damaged larynx, and various contusions. They insisted on taking me to the hospital. My head still hurt, but I was gaining mental clarity.

Simon joined me in the ambulance. He said court had been adjourned for the day. I heard him calling for police protection for me.

After a CAT scan and lots of poking and prodding, I was confined to the hospital for twenty-four hour observation. I kept insisting they check with my insurance company before they did anything.

Simon came to my room with a bouquet. "I'm so sorry, Maddy. I can't leave you alone for a minute."

"We're not going to start going to the bathroom together." I told him how everything had played out to the best of my memory which wasn't too good. I tried to think of anything I should have noticed about the cleaning woman. I was pretty sure she had been wearing rubber gloves which wouldn't have been unusual. She had black hair and thick glasses—likely a disguise, and I wasn't even sure it was a woman.

I asked Simon to hand me my purse.

"Good Lord, what's in here?"

"I brought a book to read if we had a lot of downtime. A hardback was all I had."

Simon pulled out the book and laughed. "This murder mystery probably saved your life."

"Thank God for Rita Mae Brown."

Detective Byrd arrived and we brought him up to date. His phone rang and he answered. "Yeah, what? I'll be right there."

"This might be a break," he said. "Delivery truck t-boned a rental car racing for the interstate ramp. Driver's out cold, but there are weapons in the trunk."

He looked at Simon. "Do you want to come with me?"

Simon was holding my hand and hesitated, checking to see my reaction.

"Go," I said. "Anything to end this madness."

He leaned over and kissed me gently on the one place on my cheek that wasn't bruised. "I'll be back soon."

FORTY

I DOZED OFF and on between checks. When a nurse helped me up to use the bathroom, I realized that everything hurt, not just my head. But hurting was better than dead, so I tried to be thankful.

An armed policeman or woman, depending on the shift, sat outside or in my room and scrutinized everyone coming and going, particularly the cleaning crew. Although I thought the guard might be overkill, I felt vulnerable.

I must have slept. The next thing I knew Janet sat beside me. "You awake?"

"I am now. What's going on?"

"The DA just dropped all charges against Roger. He'll be released later today. His father knows he may still be in danger and will arrange protection. And I brought your laptop."

I told her where Simon had gone and that I hadn't heard back from him. At that moment he chose to join us. He handed me a cold Diet Coke. "How are we this morning?"

"Hungry. And sore. And curious. What did you find out?"

"The gentleman from the car is still unconscious. Carrying a Maryland driver's license, but there was a Korean passport in the trunk. An Asian fellow, average height, very thin, might make jockey weight."

I had a thought. "Hand me the computer." I took a sip of caffeine, logged in to the hospital Wi-Fi and began to search South Korean newspaper sports for horseracing results. I knew Simon had already searched several countries' Jockey Club listings but the name the Asian jockey used in Ireland didn't appear. Now I was looking for a face.

My breakfast came, but I didn't stop. Finally, I saw a winner's circle photo with a jockey trying to turn away from the camera. I was pretty sure I knew that profile. "Simon, here, I think I found him."

Simon took a picture of the page with his phone and texted it to Detective Byrd. "I do believe that's our crash victim. Could that have been your cleaning woman?"

I tried to picture the face with a black wig and glasses. "Maybe, but I think there was more to the costume—cheek implants or something and pale makeup."

"We have DNA from the guy himself, he bled on the airbag. But don't know if it will be on record anywhere."

A nurse came in to check my vitals. "You probably shouldn't be trying to read," she said glancing at my computer. Then she did a double-take. "Wait, you read Korean?"

I looked at her slightly almond shaped eyes and dark, straight hair. "No, do you?"

"Sure. My mother is Korean. I grew up in Seoul. My father was stationed there. He loved to go to the races. I remember this jockey. He rode for an American trainer, and there was a big controversy that he had thrown a race."

Simon stood and moved closer. "I don't suppose you remember the trainer's name?"

"No, but it was pretty big news at the time. I would think you could find it. Let me see if I can find the jockey's name." She took the laptop and sat on the edge of the chair Simon had vacated. "Here it is, Jo Jun Ho—Jo is the surname."

Simon made some notes and snapped a picture of the link on his phone. "Later, Maddy. Call me if you need me, I'll be back after I check some things." He gave me a distracted kiss on the cheek, eager to be out the door.

The nurse asked me to power down the laptop and finished checking me over. She handed me the TV remote. "Find something mindless and rest." She noticed my untouched tray. "Can you eat something?"

"I can. I was distracted." After eating cold eggs and bacon, I tried to follow her directions, but I kept thinking about the jockey. If he had ridden for Dan Shirley, there was a connection to the news planting duo. Who else had he worked for?

We needed to talk to Shirley again.

The doctor on call released me, after making sure I knew who I was, where I was, and the current president. I answered correctly and added that I hadn't voted for him. My orders were to rest and come back if I had any concerns.

I texted Simon and asked him to come get me. He replied and said Joe would pick me up and take me to join him. My clothes had dried, although they were wrinkled and bedraggled, but then so was I.

"I can't let you out of my sight," Joe said. "Simon obviously fell down on the job."

"No, but I sure did. Can we blow this joint?"

My guard alerted his minder that I was leaving the hospital. Since we were headed for police headquarters, both the guard and Lt. Byrd approved.

Joe had ditched the suit but kept the Lexus. He brought the car around and the guard waited until I was safely inside.

I would have loved a hot shower, but I was all for progress, so I limped up the stairs to Byrd's office where Simon and the detective were comparing notes. Jo, or whatever he called himself now, was still unconscious. He had entered the country with the Korean passport the police found in his trunk. Although he hadn't actually raced at Limerick, he showed up with jockey credentials. He had raced in North and South Korea as well as mainland China as Jo. His passport bore stamps from South Africa.

Jo had never been arrested, but was involved in more than one race track investigation. He had ridden for Dan Shirley in South Korea and Kentucky.

Simon theorized that Jo had delivered the diamonds to Bill in South Africa. I asked, "Was Jo the guy in the Range Rover?"

Simon spoke. "No, Will said there were two white guys."

Simon left to arrange a face-time conference with Dan Shirley. One of the FBI agents from Kentucky would be joining us.

I hurt more by the minute. I dug in my purse for some aspirin and downed it with a diet Coke from a machine.

Joe watched me. "I'm thinking you might need a shower and a bed. Let me text Simon."

"But I don't want to miss anything."

"We'll come back later. I'll see if I can get you a key from Janet."

We stopped by Janet's office and then went to her townhouse. I assured Joe I would be fine by myself. I knew that ice might be better for my injuries, but the call of a hot shower was irresistible. I stripped off my disheveled clothing and stood under the hot spray until I couldn't stand anymore. I put on my pajamas and gratefully crawled under the covers.

I didn't wake until early the next morning. Simon was dressed and on the phone. I couldn't tell if he had slept or not, but he had changed into gray slacks and a navy blazer. His black hair was freshly washed. He came and sat on the edge of the bed, gently brushed the hair off my face, and studied me.

"Shirley is under house arrest in a Dublin hotel. We have a video chat at eight. Do you want to rest here?"

I rolled over and with a moan brought myself upright. "Not if I can come. Be ready in a few." I groaned again when I saw myself in the mirror and quickly reached for my makeup bag. With a turtleneck sweater and sunglasses, my bruises weren't as obvious.

Simon looked at me critically. "Are you sure you feel up to going out?"

"Yes. Can't quit now." I was hoarse but at least I could talk. I downed aspirin with my coffee and we headed to the police department.

Lt. Byrd had a video monitor set up in the conference room. I was introduced to the FBI agent and a few detectives from Byrd's squad.

Dan Shirley's face appeared on the monitor. "Good morning, Mr. Shirley, I hope you are feeling better," Simon said. "We have a few more questions for you."

"Certainly. However I can help."

"What did you do with the diamonds that Austin gave you?"

"I took them to a pawn shop I heard about in Lexington. Didn't want too many questions."

Simon looked down at his notes. "Do you know a jockey named Jo, originally from Korea?"

Shirley looked away from the computer and squirmed in his seat. "Ah, yes. He rode for me in a race or two in South Korea."

"Any problems with those races?"

Shirley hesitated. "He was accused of throwing a race."

"Was there any truth to that accusation?"

"Yes, but it was his idea, not mine. The thing is, Austin set it up. Said he knew a Thoroughbred owner in Korea who needed a trainer. Austin said he could rig the racing forms to change the odds by planting false information about the horses. Then he placed bets accordingly."

"Who was this owner?"

"I never knew. Horses were listed as belonging to a syndicate out of Hong Kong. After the first race I understood what the jockey had done, but I was in too deep, I couldn't get out. Jo paid me the training fees in cash. I never learned who the owners were."

Shirley stopped to take a sip of water before continuing. "We had some good races and then Jo threw one for another trainer, so my horse won. Trainer was mad as hell. I was asked to leave Korea and not come back."

"Did you ever have contact with Jo again?"

"Yeah. He showed up at Keeneland. Asked me if I knew of any local muscle. I referred him to the pawn shop—I thought they had some shady connections." Shirley took a handkerchief to wipe his forehead.

"And then what happened?" Simon was making a few notes as he questioned Shirley. The conversation was being taped and both Byrd and the FBI agent typed furiously.

Shirley looked around, anywhere but at the camera. "A guy picked me up, in a black Range Rover. We met a guy at the horse park. He gave us a package. Handed it off at the mall to another guy. Then Jo called. Said that part of the shipment was missing. He wouldn't believe that I didn't know why. Said he'd have to take care of it himself."

"Jo is in custody. You'd better hope his story agrees with yours."

"I—I'm still in danger. They'll send someone else."

"Who, Mr. Shirley? Who will send someone else?" Simon asked.

"Jo has a cousin, North Korean national, owns a diamond mine in Africa, a powerful behind-the-scenes guy, I don't know his name. But they'll kill Jo before he talks."

FORTY-ONE

THE FBI AGENT had more questions. Simon stepped out of the room and motioned for me to join him in the hall. "Byrd already has a maximum security patrol guarding Jo. And let's hope that with Jo out of commission there are no more killers out there."

Simon continued, "Interpol knows who Jo's cousin is, but as long as he stays in North Korea, we can't pick him up. We have destroyed his network. At least for now."

I thought for a minute. "So, the double diamond request was a result of miscommunication or dishonor among thieves?"

"The latter, I suspect. The Lexington gang members didn't want to share their pick-up so Jo didn't receive all the diamonds—they told him they hadn't gotten the rest. The guys that the FBI picked up at Keeneland Race Track were also local muscle, hired to assist Jo. They didn't know anything and couldn't tell us anything."

"Why smuggle the diamonds in the first place? And then plant tips about them and arms smuggling?" I was still having trouble seeing the whole picture.

"The intent was to get Monkton in trouble if they were intercepted, and if not, to convert the diamonds to cash to use for paying people like Brian Eddings.

"Jo's boss's ultimate goal was global instability and the manipulation of markets for profit. Shirley and Austin's vendetta against Monkton played right into his hands."

"What tangled webs. Are you staying here?"

"Yes, I'll meet with the FBI and Byrd this afternoon. Then the people in Dublin can wrap this up without me for a few days. How about I drive you home on the weekend?" He put his arm around me and pulled me against him.

"That would be wonderful. I can get a cab back to Janet's house now." Simon walked me to the outside door and waited until my cab arrived.

I checked my phone in the cab and found I had a message to call Lord Monkton. I got him on the first try.

"Ms. Jones," he said. "I can't thank you and Simon enough for what you have done for Roger. I'm taking him back to Dublin with me tomorrow. He'll visit his mother and then he will be starting a new position editing my Dublin paper.

"I know that Commander Simon is a professional and cannot accept anything from me, but I would like to do a favor for you if I can. Please, anything that I can do."

I was about to beg off when a thought occurred to me. "There is one thing. Can I call you in a few hours?"

FORTY-TWO

SIMON WOULD BE in Charleston for the weekend. I called Dad and Sanda and explained my plans. They would be in for a lot of last minute work, but I was pretty sure they would agree. I pulled up a long range weather forecast for the weekend. Predictions were for sunny and seventy in Charleston. Then I called Jane at the farm, Lady Atterly, and my brother, Bill, before getting back to Lord Monkton.

Simon came in shortly after six, and we brought Janet up to date on everything we had learned about the case. She was thrilled to hear that Roger would be working for his father's company in Ireland. In the process of investigating Brian's murder, she had been impressed with Roger. "That young man needs a fresh start. I think he'll do well."

We crashed early since all of us were exhausted. My phone vibrated, and I sneaked into the bathroom to answer a call from Lord Monkton. He was happy to provide a flight from Ireland. Simon was snoring but my excitement kept me awake for another hour.

I went shopping while Simon finished up on Friday. We left early Saturday morning for Charleston. I told him we needed to stay with Dad and Joan for the night, and he didn't argue. I hoped everyone could keep their mouths zipped and locked.

As we drove into Charleston on Saturday afternoon, I sent text warnings to everyone. We were greeted with hugs and giggles, and I was sure Simon would suspect that something was up. But if he did, he decided to play along.

Sunday dawned warm and sunny as promised. Dad said he and Joan had errands to run and would visit soon. He gave me a huge wink when Simon wasn't looking.

Sanda asked if we could take her by a drugstore before heading out to the farm. Then she needed a notebook from Target.

"We might as well get groceries too," I said.

She looked at her watch and back up at me. "No, I want to go to the farm now. To show Simon the horse I like."

We drove directly in the main entrance, by-passing my cottage. Sanda took Simon into the barn. Jane greeted us and asked me to come with her in the four-wheeler to check on a horse in the pasture. "Does he suspect?"

"I don't know how he couldn't but he hasn't said anything."

She drove me to the cottage. A tent was set up in front, full of tables and chairs. Pots of pink azaleas flanked the tent opening.

"The flowers are wonderful. Did you do that?" I asked.

"Your stepmother brought them out yesterday morning. And she made sure everything they did was okay with me. Nice folks you have. I'll run and change clothes and be back in a jiffy."

Jane wore mascara, lipstick, and earrings, something I had never seen before. "Thanks, Jane, you have been so good to me." I gave her a squeeze before I climbed out of the ATV.

Bill and Lady Atterly met me with hugs. She wore the scarf I had given her for Christmas over the shoulders of a well-tailored navy suit. Her salt and pepper hair was pulled back under a navy hat. Bill wore khakis, a blazer, and light blue oxford shirt.

Dad came down the stairs wearing a handsome navy suit.

"Quick, Maddy, get dressed. Sanda will only be able to stall him for so long."

My new pale pink dress lay across my bed. Joan brought in my cosmetic case. "Can I help, or do you want to be alone?"

"Please stay. I'm so excited I'm liable to go out half-dressed."

I added to my makeup and she helped me pull my hair into a casual up-do. I stepped into white sandals. My stepmother was a keeper.

"Perfect," she said. "I'll tell your dad that you're ready."

I walked to the front window. Joe had arrived, wearing his suit and holding the trumpet that I only recently learned he could play. He nodded to me, then walked out to meet Simon's approaching car. I saw him point toward the tent as he spoke to Simon. They opened the trunk, and Simon rummaged in his luggage for a blazer and tie. They walked around the back of the house.

A few minutes later, they came back, Simon straightening his tie as Dad took him to the officiant. Sanda ran up the porch stairs toward her room, peeling off clothes as she went. Joan followed to help her dress. The teenager appeared in a few minutes, tottering on spike heels, despite her leg, and looking beautiful in a pale green dress, her black hair pinned back with flower blossoms.

Joe gave a trumpet call, and Dad and I descended the front steps. Simon raised his eyebrows, Groucho Marx-like, and stepped forward from the front of the tent.

Before I knew it, the brief ceremony was over and my brother was pouring champagne for everyone. Lady Atterly was taking pictures, and I motioned to Sanda to come and stand with us. She had already ditched her heels and I was about to do the same.

Sla'inte.

Turn the page for an exciting preview of the cozy mystery...

Dead on the Trail

Working on a professional horse farm is a dream come true for Molly and John Lewis. Until the day Molly discovers a dead body near the farm...

Dead on the Trail

SHADOWS GREW DARKER under the trees, and Molly realized it was time to get back to her evening chores. Bingo began to yelp somewhere ahead of her. Kip, her big gray gelding, raised his head, sniffed, and froze. Molly could feel that he wanted to turn and flee, but she shortened the reins and he stood. She, too, could smell something decayed and suspected there was probably a dead deer just off the trail, but Bingo would normally be rolling in it, not barking. She dismounted and led Kip toward the barking dog. Bingo stood a few feet back from an upended boot. The boot was attached to a blue-jeaned leg, and the rest of a body, she presumed, but the body was covered with leaves and pretty surely dead.

Finding dead animals was part of farming, but humans were a different story. The stench was bad, but bearable, so the body must have been there for a while. Molly's stomach dropped, and she and Kip were both trembling. Focus, breathe. Get to the phone in the barn. She called Bingo and led Kip away so he would stand for her to mount. Not happening. Kip wanted out now.

"Whoa, Kip." Pulling his head around to face a thicket, she pulled her petite frame into the saddle, her earlier exhaustion replaced with adrenaline fueled urgency. Kip was eager to escape the scary smell and trotted quickly, breaking into a canter as they headed uphill. She slowed him just outside the barn, then swung off and led him to the phone mounted on the wall midway down the barn aisle.

"I want to report a body. My name is Molly Lewis.... Yes, I'm pretty sure it was dead, it certainly smelled dead, but I was holding my horse and I couldn't get closer. It's at Marsa Farm, at the end of Pearlman Farm Rd... No, it's not at any of the houses, it's in the woods, on the trail near the Broad River... My husband and I are the farm managers... No, I am not in sight of the body, because if I were I couldn't be calling you. There is no cell phone reception out here. I'll be in front of the barn, just tell them to come down the drive, the paved part dead ends at the barn."

The dispatcher assured her that a deputy was on his way and the sheriff would come out to the farm as soon as they located him. The phone rang as she hung up. Her husband, John, was calling from California. He had flown from Charlotte that morning to judge a horse show on the West Coast.

"Hey, Molly, how is everything?"

Molly began to pace up and down the barn, running her fingers through disheveled short hair. "The horses are okay, but I just found a body in the woods and—"

"Wait, did you say a body? A dead body? Do you know who it is? What were you doing in the woods?"

"Let me start at the beginning. Sam called in sick, so I had to clean the stalls and work the horses myself, then I decided to take Kip on a trail ride. Bingo started barking, and led me to the body. I just now called 911 and I still have to feed and bring in horses, and deal with the sheriff, and I don't know who it is, I just saw a leg and a boot."

"Molly, I'm sorry. What's wrong with Sam? Is he coming to work tomorrow?"

"I think so, he thought it was just a 24 hour bug." "Where's the body?"

"It's down by the river just past the turnoff to the hayfield. I think he's been dead for days, it really did stink. I'd better get off the phone, the sheriff will be here any minute, and I have to put Kip up and feed and..."

"Take it easy, honey, take your time. Do you want me to see if they can get someone else to judge so I can fly home?"

"No, John, I can cope. It took too long for you to get a judging job like this. I'm just tired and rattled. But I'll be fine. Sam will be back to work tomorrow and we can keep up with everything until you get home."

"Are you sure?"

"Yeah, I'd better go, I hear sirens. Love you." "Call me if you need me, love you."

Molly was still shaking as she unsaddled Kip. He was hot from the run up the hill so she left him cross tied in his stall, putting a light cooler over him to ward off the evening chill. An ambulance and a Barnes County Sheriff's Department car skidded to a stop in front of the barn. She called Bingo and locked him in the office before walking out to meet the deputy.

"Are you Molly? I think I met you before. I'm Deputy Frank. You found a body? Where is it?"

"It's down by the river. We probably need to take the John Deere Gator into the woods. You can drive to the bottom hay field in your car, if you've got four wheel drive, but the body's in the woods off the trail." The Gator started on the second try, a record, and she led him down the hill, with the ambulance following. Shivering, she reached behind the seat looking for a jacket or sweatshirt, but there was nothing but baling twine and an empty feed bucket. The deputy parked at the edge of the hayfield and joined Molly in the ATV. The paramedics sat in the cargo area. They entered the trail and turned right along the river. She slowed, searching ahead in the growing darkness. Her headlights hit a broad tree trunk and she stopped, backing up and aiming the lights into the woods on her left. The deputy turned on his flashlight, scanning the ground where she pointed.

"The body's right over there, you'll see a boot sticking out of the leaves."

The deputy and the ambulance attendants motioned her to stand back as they uncovered the body. She gladly complied, not wanting to look, yet compelled by curiosity. Molly hoped it would be an unknown person, dead of natural causes. But life, and now death, at Marsa Farm, was never that simple. When she saw the grey pony tail she knew she was right. The bloody bullet hole in his chest pretty much ruled out natural causes. And she didn't see a gun in his hand. He was trouble alive and she suspected he might be more trouble dead.

Deputy Frank walked back to her, "Do you know who this is?"

"I think so—"

Deputy Frank picked up his radio.

Acknowledgements

American Saddlebred horses have been exported to South Africa since 1917. The first export was a black stallion, Meyer's Kentucky Star. My father, L. Herbert Sullivan, owned and sold the stallion Edgeview King (originally registered as Juan Rex) to South Africa after he was Reserve World Champion Junior Five-Gaited Horse circa 1940 with Kenny Carson. Edgeview King's picture hangs above my desk.

In the 1990s South African horses began coming back to the USA. Bill Schoeman imported Commander in Chief in 1995. Since then, many great horses and many fine horsemen have come to America from South Africa. Dorian's Wild Temper and his offspring are descendants of Edgeview King.

In the 1970s, Lee Kaplan wrote a book about the American Saddlebred in South Africa. I couldn't afford a copy but the author wrote to me saying, "...had Juan Rex been my horse no money could have bought him. In my opinion he was the greatest horse ever to come into South Africa and has left an indelible stamp on the breed in this country." I framed the letter and gave it to my father.

I thank my critique groups, past and present, Carol, Mary Ann, Sheila, Peter, Cindy, Elizabeth, Sharon, Barbara, Dave, and Chris for all of your helpful criticism and encouragement. My editor and publisher, Narielle Living, deserves my appreciation for all that she does. Winston-Salem Writers and Chesapeake Bay Writers organizations provide climates conducive to writing. My sister-in-law, Shirley North, helped me with a few Irish details and any mistakes are mine, not hers. I have also taken some liberty with Irish geography, but this is a work of fiction.

My husband, Wallace, lovingly supports and puts up with a writer. Our dog, Remi, is usually sprawled out in my office as I write. And I thank all of my family and friends for love of all things horse.

About the Author

Susan Williamson grew up on a horse, cattle, hog and sheep farm in Western Pennsylvania. She completed a BS in Agriculture from the University of Kentucky and earned an MS from the University of California, Davis. After meeting at a horse show, she and her husband raised their family in rural Kentucky before moving to North Carolina to operate a horse training, breeding, lesson and boarding farm. She has been an extension agent, newspaper editor, educator, food coop manager, and professional horsewoman. She is the author of two novels: *Desert Tail* and *Dead on the Trail.* She currently resides in Williamsburg, VA with her husband and Labradoodle and is a contributor to *Next Door Neighbors* and *Tidewater Women* magazines.

CPSIA information can be obtained
at www.ICGtesting.com
Printed in the USA
LVHW020934191020
669133LV00011B/457